T0019252

Cindy Lee Johnson

DENIS JOHNSON is the author of six novels, three collections of poetry, and one book of reportage. His novel *Tree of Smoke* was the 2007 winner of the National Book Award.

ALSO BY DENIS JOHNSON

FICTION

NONFICTION

POETRY

PLAYS

"No other book engaged the full capacities of my intellect, emotion, and imagination. . . . This book had a profound effect on me—after I'd read the final words of *Train Dreams,* I felt as if I'd been gifted something ancient and true, and immediately opened the book to page one and began to read it again."

—Alan Heathcock, *Salon*

"Renders the story of America and our westward course of empire in the most beautiful and heartbreaking manner imaginable . . . An intense and rewarding reading experience."

—Andrew Ervin, *The Miami Herald*

"Recalls Cormac McCarthy and nods to Bret Harte . . . much of the pleasure in reading *Train Dreams* comes from the luxurious exactitude of Johnson's writing. . . . It palpably conjures the beauty of an American West then still very much a place of natural wonder and menace, and places one man's lonely life in that landscape, where he's at once comfortably at home and utterly lost." —Dan DeLuca, *The Philadelphia Inquirer*

"A calm, measured stunner from a master of sentences."

—*Austin American-Statesman,* Best Books of 2011

"Think of the spare straight lines of a Grant Wood engraving. Denis Johnson's striking new short novel about life, fate, and death in the early twentieth-century American mountain West, leaves that impression—plain yet stark in its depiction of an ordinary man's life both particular and universal." —Alan Cheuse, NPR

"The density of historical detail, the meticulous chronicling of logging and bridge building, flora and fauna of the American West, which make for an otherworldly atmospheric richness . . . What is this *about*? I kept asking myself as I read. . . . The real answer is something much larger, I think, suggested only in the most glancing ways until the devastating last line: the cataclysmic changes wrought by the twentieth century, and the corollary disappearance of a certain kind of American life." —Jennifer Egan

"A sweeping tall tale, an homage to Bret Harte, a work of North American magical realism, a yarn of the supernatural variety . . . Its power lies in its visitations, its haunted moments of sadness and yearning in which the world appears otherworldly and aggrieved even while infused with comedy." —David Guterson

TRAIN

DREAMS

DENIS JOHNSON

PICADOR

FARRAR, STRAUS AND GIROUX
NEW YORK

This novella was originally published, in slightly different form,
in *The Paris Review*, 2002.

www.picadorusa.com
www.twitter.com/picadorusa • www.facebook.com/picadorusa

Picador® is a U.S. registered trademark and is used by Farrar, Straus and Giroux
under license from Pan Books Limited.

For book club information, please visit www.facebook.com/picadorbookclub
or e-mail marketing@picadorusa.com.

Designed by Jonathan D. Lippincott

The Library of Congress has cataloged the Farrar, Straus and Giroux edition as follows:

Johnson, Denis, 1949–
Train dreams / Denis Johnson. — 1st ed.
p. cm.
ISBN 978-0-374-28114-4
PS3560.O3745T73 2011
813'.54—dc22

2011007505

Picador ISBN 978-1-250-00765-0

First published in the United States by Farrar, Straus and Giroux

First Picador Edition: June 2012

30 29 28 27 26

for Cindy Lee forever

TRAIN DREAMS

1

In the summer of 1917 Robert Grainier took part in an attempt on the life of a Chinese laborer caught, or anyway accused of, stealing from the company stores of the Spokane International Railway in the Idaho Panhandle.

Three of the railroad gang put the thief under restraint and dragged him up the long bank toward the bridge under construction fifty feet above the Moyea River. A rapid singsong streamed from the Chinaman voluminously. He shipped and twisted like a weasel in a sack, lashing backward with his one free fist at the man lugging him by the neck. As this group passed him, Grainier, seeing them in some distress, lent assistance and found himself holding one of the culprit's bare feet. The man facing him, Mr. Sears, of Spokane International's management, held the prisoner almost uselessly by the armpit and was the only one of them, besides the incomprehensible Chinaman, to talk during the hardest part of their labors: "Boys, I'm damned if we ever see the top of this heap!" Then we're hauling him all the way? was the question Grainier wished to ask, but he thought it better to save his breath for the struggle. Sears laughed once, his face pale with fatigue and horror. They all went down in the dust and got righted, went down again, the Chinaman speaking in tongues and terrifying the four of them to the point that whatever they may have had in mind at the outset, he was a deader now. Nothing would do but to toss him off the trestle.

They came abreast of the others, a gang of a dozen men pausing in the sun to lean on their tools and wipe at sweat and watch this thing. Grainier held on convulsively to the Chinaman's horny foot, wondering at himself, and the man with the other foot let loose and sat down gasping in the dirt and got himself kicked in the eye before Grainier took charge of the free-flailing limb. "It was just for fun. For fun," the man sitting in the dirt said, and to his confederate there he said, "Come on, Jel Toomis, let's give it up." "I can't let loose," this Mr. Toomis said, "I'm the one's got him by the neck!" and laughed with a gust of confusion passing across his features. "Well, I've got him!" Grainier said, catching both the little demon's feet tighter in his embrace. "I've got the bastard, and I'm your man!"

The party of executioners got to the midst of the last completed span, sixty feet above the rapids, and made every effort to toss the Chinaman over. But he bested them by clinging to their arms and legs, weeping his gibberish, until suddenly he let go and grabbed the beam beneath him with one hand. He kicked free of his captors easily, as they were trying to shed themselves of him anyway, and went over the side, dangling over the gorge and making hand-over-hand out over the river on the skeleton form of the next span. Mr. Toomis's companion rushed over now, balancing on a beam, kicking at the fellow's fingers. The Chinaman dropped from beam to beam like a circus artist downward along the crosshatch structure. A couple of the work gang cheered his escape, while others, though not quite certain why he was being chased, shouted that the villain ought to be stopped. Mr. Sears removed from the holster on his belt a large old four-shot black-powder revolver and took his four, to no effect. By then the Chinaman had vanished.

•

Hiking to his home after this incident, Grainier detoured two miles to the store at the railroad village of Meadow Creek to get a bottle of Hood's Sarsaparilla for his wife, Gladys, and their infant daughter, Kate. It was hot going up the hill through the woods toward the cabin, and before getting the last mile he stopped and bathed in the river, the Moyea, at a deep place upstream from the village.

It was Saturday night, and in preparation for the evening a number of the railroad gang from Meadow Creek were gathered at the hole, bathing with their clothes on and sitting themselves out on the rocks to dry before the last of the daylight left the canyon. The men left their shoes and boots aside and waded in slowly up to their shoulders, whooping and splashing. Many of the men already sipped whiskey from flasks as they sat shivering after their ablutions. Here and there an arm and hand clutching a shabby hat jutted from the surface while somebody got his head wet. Grainier recognized nobody and stayed off by himself and kept a close eye on his boots and his bottle of sarsaparilla.

Walking home in the falling dark, Grainier almost met the Chinaman everywhere. Chinaman in the road. Chinaman in the woods. Chinaman walking softly, dangling his hands on arms like ropes. Chinaman dancing up out of the creek like a spider.

•

He gave the Hood's to Gladys. She sat up in bed by the stove, nursing the baby at her breast, down with a case of the salt rheum. She could easily have braved it and done her washing and cut up potatoes and trout for supper, but it was their custom to let her lie up with a bottle or two of the sweet-tasting Hood's tonic when her head ached and her nose stopped, and get a holiday from such chores. Grainier's baby daughter, too, looked rheumy. Her eyes were a bit crusted and the discharge bubbled pendulously at her nostrils while she suckled and snorted at her mother's breast. Kate was four months old, still entirely bald. She did not seem to recognize him. Her little illness wouldn't hurt her as long as she didn't develop a cough out of it.

Now Grainier stood by the table in the single-room

cabin and worried. The Chinaman, he was sure, had cursed them powerfully while they dragged him along, and any bad thing might come of it. Though astonished now at the frenzy of the afternoon, baffled by the violence, at how it had carried him away like a seed in a wind, young Grainier still wished they'd gone ahead and killed that Chinaman before he'd cursed them.

He sat on the edge of the bed.

"Thank you, Bob," his wife said.

"Do you like your sarsaparilla?"

"I do. Yes, Bob."

"Do you suppose little Kate can taste it out your teat?"

"Of course she can."

·

Many nights they heard the northbound Spokane International train as it passed through Meadow Creek, two miles down the valley. Tonight the distant whistle woke him, and he found himself alone in the straw bed.

Gladys was up with Kate, sitting on the bench by the stove, scraping cold boiled oats off the sides of the pot and letting the baby suckle this porridge from the end of her finger.

"How much does she know, do you suppose, Gladys? As much as a dog-pup, do you suppose?"

"A dog-pup can live by its own after the bitch weans it away," Gladys said.

He waited for her to explain what this meant. She often thought ahead of him.

"A man-child couldn't do that way," she said, "just go off and live after it was weaned. A dog knows more than a babe until the babe knows its words. But not just a few words. A dog raised around the house knows some words, too—as many as a baby."

"How many words, Gladys?"

"You know," she said, "the words for its tricks and the things you tell it to do."

"Just say some of the words, Glad." It was dark and he wanted to keep hearing her voice.

"Well, fetch, and come, and sit, and lay, and roll over. Whatever it knows to do, it knows the words."

In the dark he felt his daughter's eyes turned on him like a cornered brute's. It was only his thoughts tricking him, but it poured something cold down his spine. He shuddered and pulled the quilt up to his neck.

All of his life Robert Grainier was able to recall this very moment on this very night.

2

Forty-one days later, Grainier stood among the railroad gang and watched while the first locomotive crossed the 112-foot interval of air over the 60-foot-deep gorge, traveling on the bridge they'd made. Mr. Sears stood next to the machine, a single engine, and raised his four-shooter to signal the commencement. At the sound of the gun the engineer tripped the brake and hopped out of the contraption, and the men shouted it on as it trudged very slowly over the tracks and across the Moyea to the other side, where a second man waited to jump aboard and halt it before it ran out of track. The men cheered and whooped. Grainier felt sad. He couldn't think why. He cheered and hollered too. The structure would be called Eleven-Mile Cutoff Bridge because it eliminated a long curve around the gorge and through an adjacent pass and saved the Spokane International's having to look after that eleven-mile stretch of rails and ties.

•

Grainier's experience on the Eleven-Mile Cutoff made him hungry to be around other such massive undertakings, where swarms of men did away with portions of the forest and assembled structures as big as anything going, knitting massive wooden trestles in the air of impassable chasms, always bigger, longer, deeper. He went to northwestern Washington in 1920 to help make repairs on the Robinson Gorge Bridge, the grandest yet. The conceivers of these schemes had managed to bridge a space 208 feet deep and 804 feet wide with a railway capable of supporting an engine and two flatcars of logs. The Robinson Gorge Bridge was nearly thirty years old, wobbly and terrifying—nobody ever rode the cars across, not even the engineer. The brakeman caught it at the other end.

When the repairs were done, Grainier moved higher

into the forest with the Simpson Company and worked getting timber out. A system of brief corduroy roads worked all over the area. The rails were meant only for transporting timber out of the forest; it was the job of the forty-some-odd men whom Grainier had joined to get the logs by six-horse teams within cable's reach of the railway landing.

At the landing crouched a giant engine the captain called a donkey, an affair with two tremendous iron drums, one paying out cable and the other winding it in, dragging logs to the landing and sending out the hook simultaneously to the choker, who noosed the next log. The engine was an old wood-burning steam colossus throbbing and booming and groaning while its vapors roared like a falls, the horses over on the skid road moving gigantically in a kind of silence, their noises erased by the commotion of steam and machinery. From the landing the logs went onto railroad flatcars, and then across the wondrous empty depth of Robinson Gorge and down the mountain to the link with all the railways of the American continent.

Meanwhile Robert Grainier had passed his thirty-fifth birthday. He missed Gladys and Kate, his Li'l Girl and Li'l Li'l Girl, but he'd lived thirty-two years a bachelor before finding a wife, and easily slipped back into a steadying loneliness out here among the countless spruce.

Grainier himself served as a choker—not on the landing, but down in the woods, where sawyers labored in pairs to fell the spruce, limbers worked with axes to get them clean, and buckers cut them into eighteen-foot lengths before the chokers looped them around with cable to be hauled out by the horses. Grainier relished the work, the straining, the heady exhaustion, the deep rest at the end of the day. He liked the grand size of things in the woods, the feeling of being lost and far away, and the sense he had that with so many trees as wardens, no danger could find him. But according to one of the fellows, Arn Peeples, an old man now, formerly a jim-crack sawyer, the trees themselves were killers, and while a good sawyer might judge ninety-nine times correctly how a fall would go, and even by remarkable cuts and wedging tell a fifty-tonner to swing around uphill and light behind him as deftly as a needle, the hundredth time might see him smacked in the face and deader than a rock, just like that. Arn Peeples said he'd once watched a five-ton log jump up startled and fly off the cart and tumble over six horses, killing all six. It was only when you left it alone that a tree might treat you as a friend. After the blade bit in, you had yourself a war.

Cut off from anything else that might trouble them, the gang, numbering sometimes more than forty and never fewer than thirty-five men, fought the forest from sunrise until suppertime, felling and bucking the giant spruce into pieces of a barely manageable size, accomplishing labors, Grainier sometimes thought, tantamount to the pyramids, changing the face of the mountainsides, talking little, shouting their communications, living with the sticky feel of pitch in their beards, sweat washing the dust off their long johns and caking it in the creases of their necks and joints, the odor of pitch so thick it abraded their throats and stung their eyes, and even overlaid the stink of beasts and manure. At day's end the gang slept nearly where they fell. A few rated cabins. Most stayed in tents: These were ancient affairs patched extensively with burlap, most of them; but their canvas came originally from infantry tents of the Civil War, on the Union side, according to Arn Peeples. He pointed out stains of blood on the fabric. Some of these tents had gone on to house U.S. Cavalry in the Indian campaigns, serving longer, surely, than any they sheltered, so reckoned Arn Peeples.

"Just let me at that hatchet, boys," he liked to say. "When I get to chopping, you'll come to work in the morning and the chips won't yet be settled from yesterday . . .

"I'm made for this summer logging," said Arn Peeples. "You Minnesota fellers might like to complain about it. I don't get my gears turning smooth till it's over a hundred. I worked on a peak outside Bisbee, Arizona, where we were only eleven or twelve miles from the sun. It was a hundred and sixteen degrees on the thermometer, and every degree was a foot long. And that was in the shade. And there wasn't no shade." He called all his logging comrades "Minnesota fellers." As far as anybody could ascertain, nobody among them had ever laid eyes on Minnesota.

Arn Peeples had come up from the Southwest and claimed to have seen and spoken to the Earp brothers in Tombstone; he described the famous lawmen as "crazy trash." He'd worked in Arizona mines in his youth, then sawed all over logging country for decades, and now he was a frail and shrunken gadabout, always yammering, staying out of the way of hard work, the oldest man in the woods.

His real use was occasional. When a tunnel had to be excavated, he served as the powder monkey, setting charges and blasting his way deeper and deeper into a bluff until he came out the other side, men clearing away the rubble for him after each explosion. He was a superstitious person and did each thing exactly the way he'd done it in the Mule Mountains in south Arizona, in the copper mines.

"I witnessed Mr. John Jacob Warren lose his entire fortune. Drunk and said he could outrun a horse." This might have been true. Arn Peeples wasn't given to lying, at least didn't make claims to know many famous figures, other than the Earps, and, in any case, nobody up here had heard of any John Jacob Warren. "Wagered he could outrun a three-year-old stallion! Stood in the street swaying back and forth with his eyes crossed, that drunk, I mean to say—the richest man in Arizona!— and he took off running with that stallion's butt end looking at him all the way. Bet the whole Copper Queen Mine. And lost it, too! *There's* a feller I'd like to gamble with! Of course he's busted down to his drop-bottoms now, and couldn't make a decent wager."

Sometimes Peeples set a charge, turned the screw to set it off, and got nothing for his trouble. Then a general tension and silence gripped the woods. Men working half a mile away would somehow get an understanding that a dud charge had to be dealt with, and all work stopped. Peeples would empty his pockets of his few valuables—a brass watch, a tin comb, and a silver toothpick—lay them on a stump, and proceed into the darkness of his tunnel without looking back. When he came out and turned his screws again and the dynamite blew with a whomp, the men cheered and a cloud of dust rushed from the tunnel and powdered rock came raining down over everyone.

It looked certain Arn Peeples would exit this world in a puff of smoke with a monstrous noise, but he went out quite differently, hit across the back of his head by a dead branch falling off a tall larch—the kind of snag called a "widowmaker" with just this kind of misfortune in mind. The blow knocked him silly, but he soon came around and seemed fine, complaining only that his spine felt "knotty amongst the knuckles" and "I want to walk suchways—crooked." He had a number of dizzy spells and grew dreamy and forgetful over the course of the next few days, lay up all day Sunday racked with chills and fever, and on Monday morning was found in his bed deceased, with the covers up under his chin and "such a sight of comfort," as the captain said, "that you'd just as soon not disturb him—just lower him down into a great long wide grave, bed and all." Arn Peeples had said a standing tree might be a friend, but it was from just such a tree that his death had descended.

Arn's best friend, Billy, also an old man, but generally wordless, mustered a couple of remarks by the grave mound: "Arn Peeples never cheated a man in his life," he said. "He never stole, not even a stick of candy when he was a small, small boy, and he lived to be pretty old. I guess there's a lesson in there for all of us to be square, and we'll all get along. In Jesus' name, amen." The others said, "Amen." "I wish I could let us all lay off a day," the captain said. "But it's the company, and it's the war." The war in Europe had created a great demand for spruce. An armistice had actually been signed eighteen months before, but the captain believed an armistice to be only a temporary thing until the battles resumed and one side massacred the other to the last man.

That night the men discussed Arn's assets and failings and went over the details of his final hours. Had the injuries to his brain addled him, or was it the fever he'd suddenly come down with? In his delirium he'd shouted mad words—"right reverend rising rockies!" he'd shouted; "forerunner grub holdup feller! Caution! Caution!"—and called out to the spirits from his past, and said he'd been paid a visit by his sister and his sis-

ter's husband, though both, as Billy said he knew for
certain, had been many years dead.

Billy's jobs were to keep the double drum's engine
watered and lubricated and to watch the cables for
wear. This was easy work, old man's work. The outfit's
real grease monkey was a boy, twelve-year-old Harold,
the captain's son, who moved along before the teams of
horses with a bucket of dogfish oil, slathering it across
the skids with a swab of burlap to keep the huge logs
sliding. One morning, Wednesday morning, just two
days after Arn Peeples's death and burial, young Harold himself took a dizzy spell and fell over onto his
work, and the horses shied and nearly overturned the
load, trying to keep from trampling him. The boy was
saved from a mutilated death by the lucky presence of
Grainier himself, who happened to be standing aside
waiting to cross the skid road and hauled the boy out
of the way by the leg of his pants. The captain watched
over his son all afternoon, bathing his forehead with
spring water. The youth was feverish and crazy, and it
was this malady that had laid him out in front of the
big animals.

That night old Billy also took a chill and lay pitch-
ing from side to side on his cot and steadily raving until
well past midnight. Except for his remarks at his friend's

graveside, Billy probably hadn't let go of two or three words the whole time the men had known him, but now he kept the nearest ones awake, and those sleeping farther away in the camp later reported hearing from him in their dreams that night, mostly calling out his own name—"Who is it? Who's there?" he called. "Billy? Billy? Is that you, Billy?"

Harold's fever broke, but Billy's lingered. The captain acted like a man full of haunts, wandering the camp and bothering the men, catching one whenever he could and poking his joints, thumbing back his eyelids and prying apart his jaws like a buyer of livestock. "We're finished for the summer," he told the men Friday night as they lined up for supper. He'd calculated each man's payoff—Grainier had sent money home all summer and still had four hundred dollars coming to him.

By Sunday night they had the job shut up and the last logs down the mountain, and six more men had come over with chills. Monday morning the captain gave each of his workers a four-dollar bonus and said, "Get out of this place, boys." By this time Billy, too, had survived the crisis of his illness. But the captain said he feared an influenza epidemic like the one in 1897. He himself had been orphaned then, his entire family of thirteen siblings dead in a single week. Grainier felt pity for his boss. The captain had been a strong leader and a fair one, a blue-eyed, middle-aged man who trafficked little with anybody but his son Harold, and he'd never told anyone he'd grown up without any family.

This was Grainier's first summer in the woods, and the Robinson Gorge was the first of several railroad bridges he worked on. Years later, many decades later, in fact, in 1962 or 1963, he watched young ironworkers on a trestle where U.S. Highway 2 crossed the Moyea River's deepest gorge, every bit as long and deep as the Robinson. The old highway took a long detour to cross at a shallow place; the new highway shot straight across the chasm, several hundred feet above the river. Grainier marveled at the youngsters swiping each other's hard hats and tossing them down onto the safety net thirty or forty feet below, jumping down after them to bounce crazily in the netting, clambering up its strands back to the wooden catwalk. He'd been a regular chimpanzee on the girders himself, but now he couldn't get up on a high stool without feeling just a little queasy. As he watched them, it occurred to him that he'd lived almost eighty years and had seen the world turn and turn.

Some years earlier, in the mid-1950s, Grainier had paid ten cents to view the World's Fattest Man, who rested on a divan in a trailer that took him from town to town. To get the World's Fattest Man onto this divan they'd had to take the trailer's roof off and lower him down with a crane. He weighed in at just over a thousand pounds. There he sat, immense and dripping sweat, with a mustache and goatee and one gold earring like a pirate's, wearing shiny gold short pants and nothing else, his flesh rolling out on either side of him from one end of the divan to the other and spilling over and dangling toward the floor like an arrested waterfall, while out of this big pile of himself poked his head and arms and legs. People waited in line to stand at the open doorway and look in. He told each one to buy a picture of him from a stack by the window there for a dime.

Later in his long life Grainier confused the chronology of the past and felt certain that the day he'd viewed the World's Fattest Man—that evening—was the very same day he stood on Fourth Street in Troy, Montana, twenty-six miles east of the bridge, and looked at a railway car carrying the strange young hillbilly entertainer Elvis Presley. Presley's private train had stopped for some reason, maybe for repairs, here in this little town that didn't even merit its own station. The famous youth had appeared in a window briefly and raised his hand in greeting, but Grainier had come out of the barbershop across the street too late to see this. He'd only had it told to him by the townspeople standing in the late dusk, strung along the street beside the deep bass of the idling diesel, speaking very low if speaking at all, staring into the mystery and grandeur of a boy so high and solitary.

Grainier had also once seen a wonder horse, and a wolf-boy, and he'd flown in the air in a biplane in 1927. He'd started his life story on a train ride he couldn't remember, and ended up standing around outside a train with Elvis Presley in it.

3

When a child, Grainier had been sent by himself to Idaho. From precisely where he'd been sent he didn't know, because his eldest cousin said one thing and his second-eldest another, and he himself couldn't remember. His second-eldest cousin also claimed not to be his cousin at all, while the first said yes, they were cousins—their mother, whom Grainier thought of as his own mother as much as theirs, was actually his aunt, the sister of his father. All three of his cousins agreed Grainier had come on a train. How had he lost his original parents? Nobody ever told him.

When he disembarked in the town of Fry, Idaho, he

was six—or possibly seven, as it seemed a long time since his last birthday and he thought he may have missed the date, and couldn't say, anyhow, where it fell. As far as he could ever fix it, he'd been born sometime in 1886, either in Utah or in Canada, and had found his way to his new family on the Great Northern Railroad, the building of which had been completed in 1893. He arrived after several days on the train with his destination pinned to his chest on the back of a store receipt. He'd eaten all of his food the first day of his travels, but various conductors had kept him fed along the way. The whole adventure made him forget things as soon as they happened, and he very soon misplaced this earliest part of his life entirely. His eldest cousin, a girl, said he'd come from northeast Canada and had spoken only French when they'd first seen him, and they'd had to whip the French out of him to get room for the English tongue. The other two cousins, both boys, said he was a Mormon from Utah. At so early an age it never occurred to him to find out from his aunt and uncle who he was. By the time he thought to ask them, many years had passed and they'd long since died, both of them.

His earliest memory was that of standing beside his uncle Robert Grainier, the First, standing no higher than the elbow of this smoky-smelling man he'd quickly got to calling Father, in the mud street of Fry within sight of the Kootenai River, observing the mass deportation of a hundred or more Chinese families from the town. Down at the street's end, at the Bonner Lumber Company's railroad yard, men with axes, pistols, and shotguns in their hands stood by saying very little while the strange people clambered onto three flatcars, jabbering like birds and herding their children into the midst of themselves, away from the edges of the open cars. The small, flat-faced men sat on the outside of the three groups, their knees drawn up and their hands locked around their shins, as the train left Fry and headed away to someplace it didn't occur to Grainier to wonder about until decades later, when he was a grown man and had come very near killing a Chinaman—had wanted to kill him. Most had ended up thirty or so miles west, in Montana, between the towns of Troy and Libby, in a place beside the Kootenai River that came to be called China Basin. By the time Grainier was working on bridges, the community had dispersed, and only a few lived here and there in the area, and nobody was afraid of them anymore.

The Kootenai River flowed past Fry as well. Grainier had patchy memories of a week when the water broke over its banks and flooded the lower portion of Fry. A few of the frailest structures washed away and broke apart downstream. The post office was undermined and carried off, and Grainier remembered being lifted up by somebody, maybe his father, and surfacing above the heads of a large crowd of townspeople to watch the building sail away on the flood. Afterward some Canadians found the post office stranded on the lowlands one hundred miles downriver in British Columbia.

Robert and his new family lived in town. Only two doors away a bald man, always in a denim oversuit, always hatless—a large man, with very small, strong hands—kept a shop where he mended boots. Sometimes when he was out of sight little Robert or one of his cousins liked to nip in and rake out a gob of beeswax from the mason jar of it on his workbench. The mender used it to wax his thread when he sewed on tough leather, but the children sucked at it like candy.

The mender, for his part, chewed tobacco like many folks. One day he caught the three neighbor children as they passed his door. "Look here," he said. He bent over and expectorated half a mouthful into a glass canning jar nestled up against the leg of his table. He picked up this receptacle and swirled the couple inches of murky spit it held. "You children want a little taste out of this?"

They didn't answer.

"Go ahead and have a drink!—if you think you'd like to," he said.

They didn't answer.

He poured the horrible liquid into his jar of beeswax and glopped it all around with a finger and held the finger out toward their faces and hollered, "Take some anytime you'd like!" He laughed and laughed. He rocked in his chair, wiping his tiny fingers on his denim lap. A vague disappointment shone in his eyes as he looked around and found nobody there to tell about his maneuver.

In 1899 the towns of Fry and Eatonville were combined under the name of Bonners Ferry. Grainier got his reading and numbers at the Bonners Ferry schoolhouse. He was never a scholar, but he learned to decipher writing on a page, and it helped him to get along in the world. In his teens he lived with his eldest cousin Suzanne and her family after she married, this following the death of their parents, his aunt and uncle Helen and Robert Grainier.

He quit attending school in his early teens and,

without parents to fuss at him, became a layabout. Fishing by himself along the Kootenai one day, just a mile or so upriver from town, he came on an itinerant bum, a "boomer," as his sort was known, holed up among some birches in a sloppy camp, nursing an injured leg. "Come on up here. Please, young feller," the boomer called. "Please—please! I'm cut through the cords of my knee, and I want you to know a few things."

Young Robert wound in his line and laid the pole aside. He climbed the bank and stopped ten feet from where the man sat up against a tree with his legs out straight, barefoot, the left leg resting over a pallet of evergreen limbs. The man's old shoes lay one on either side of him. He was bearded and streaked with dust, and bits of the woods clung to him everywhere. "Rest your gaze on a murdered man," he said.

"I ain't even going to ask you to bring me a drink of water," the man said. "I'm dry as boots, but I'm going to die, so I don't think I need any favors." Robert was paralyzed. He had the impression of a mouth hole moving in a stack of leaves and rags and matted brown hair. "I've got just one or two things that must be said, or they'll go to my grave . . .

"That's right," he said. "I been cut behind the knee by this one feller they call Big-Ear Al. And I have to say, I know he's killed me. That's the first thing. Take that news to your sheriff, son. William Coswell Haley, from St. Louis, Missouri, has been robbed, cut in the leg, and murdered by the boomer they call Big-Ear Al. He snatched my roll of fourteen dollars off me whilst I slept, and he cut the strings back of my knee so's I wouldn't chase after him. My leg's stinking," he said, "because I've laid up here so long the rot's set in. You know how that'll do. That rot will travel till I'm dead right up to my eyes. Till I'm a corpse able to see things. Able to think its thoughts. Then about the fourth day I'll be all the way dead. I don't know what happens to us then——if we can think our thoughts in the grave, or we fly to Heaven, or get taken to the Devil. But here's what I have to say, just in case:

"I am William Coswell Haley, forty-two years old. I was a good man with jobs and prospects in St. Louis, Missouri, until a bit more than four years ago. At that time my niece Susan Haley became about twelve years of age, and, as I was living in my brother's house in those days, I started to get around her in her bed at night. I couldn't sleep——it got that way, I couldn't stop my heart from running and racing——until I'd got up from my pallet and snuck to the girl's room and got around her bed, and just stood there quiet. Well, she never woke. Not even one night when I rustled her covers. Another night I touched her face and she never woke, grabbed at her foot and didn't get a rise. Another night I pulled at her covers, and she was the same as dead. I touched her, lifted her shift, did every little thing I wanted. Every little thing. And she never woke.

"And that got to be my way. Night after night. Every little thing. She never woke.

"Well, I came home one day, and I'd been working at the candle factory, which was an easy job to acquire when a feller had no other. Mostly old gals working there, but they'd take anybody on. When I got to the house, my sister-in-law Alice Haley was sitting in the yard on a wet winter's day, sitting on the greasy grass. Just plunked there. Bawling like a baby.

" 'What is it, Alice?'

" 'My husband's took a stick to our little daughter Susan! My husband's took a stick to her! A stick!'

" 'Good God, is she hurt,' I said, 'or is it just her feelings?'

" 'Hurt? Hurt?' she cries at me—'My little girl is dead!'

"I didn't even go into the house. Left whatever-all I owned and walked to the railway and got on a flatcar, and I've never been a hundred yards from these train tracks ever since. Been all over this country. Canada, too. Never a hundred yards from these rails and ties.

"Little young Susan had a child in her, is what her mother told me. And her father beat on her to drive that poor child out of her belly. Beat on her till he'd killed her."

For a few minutes the dying man stopped talking. He grabbed at breaths, put his hands to the ground either side of him and seemed to want to shift his posture, but had no strength. He couldn't seem to get a decent breath in his lungs, panting and wheezing. "I'll take that drink of water now." He closed his eyes and ceased struggling for air. When Robert got near, certain the man had died, William Haley spoke without opening his eyes: "Just bring it to me in that old shoe."

4

The boy never told anyone about William Coswell Haley. Not the sheriff, or his cousin Suzanne, or anyone else. He brought the man one swallow of water in the man's own boot, and left William Haley to die alone. It was the most cowardly and selfish of the many omissions that might have been counted against him in his early years. But maybe the incident affected him in a way nobody could have traced, because Robert Grainier settled in and worked through the rest of his youth as one of the labor pool around town, hiring out to the railroad or to the entrepreneurial families of the area, the Eatons, the Frys, or the Bonners, finding work on the crews pretty well whenever he needed, because he stayed away from drink or anything unseemly and was known as a steady man.

He worked around town right through his twenties—a man of whom it might have been said, but nothing was ever said of him, that he had little to interest him. At thirty-one he still chopped firewood, loaded trucks, served among various gangs formed up by more enterprising men for brief jobs here and there.

Then he met Gladys Olding. One of his cousins, later he couldn't remember which one to thank, took him to church with the Methodists, and there she was, a small girl just across the aisle from him, who sang softly during the hymns in a voice he picked out without any trouble. A session of lemonade and pastries followed the service, and there in the courtyard she introduced herself to him casually, with an easy smile, as if girls did things like that every day, and maybe they did—Robert Grainier didn't know, as Robert Grainier stayed away from girls. Gladys looked much older than her years, having grown up, she explained to him, in a house in a sunny pasture, and having spent too much time in the summer light. Her hands were as rough as any fifty-year-old man's.

They saw each other frequently, Grainier forced, by

the nature of their friendship, to seek her out almost always at the Methodist Sunday services and at the Wednesday night prayer group. When the summer was full-on, Grainier took her by the River Road to show her the acre he'd acquired on the short bluff above the Moyea. He'd bought it from young Glenwood Fry, who had wanted an automobile and who eventually got one by selling many small parcels of land to other young people. He told her he'd try some gardening here. The nicest place for a cabin lay just down a path from a sparsely overgrown knoll he could easily level by moving around the stones it was composed of. He could clear a bigger area cutting logs for a cabin, and pulling at stumps wouldn't be urgent, as he'd just garden among them, to start. A half-mile path through a thick woods led into a meadow cleared some years back by Willis Grossling, now deceased. Grossling's daughter had said Grainier could graze a few animals there as long as he didn't run a real herd over the place. Anyway he didn't want more than a couple sheep and a couple goats. Maybe a milk cow. Grainier explained all this to Gladys without explaining why he was explaining. He hoped she guessed. He thought she must, because for this outing she'd put on the same dress she usually wore to church.

This was on a hot June day. They'd borrowed a wagon from Gladys's father and brought a picnic in two baskets. They hiked over to Grossling's meadow and waded into it through daisies up to their knees. They put out a blanket beside a seasonal creek trickling over the grass and lay back together. Grainier considered the pasture a beautiful place. Somebody should paint it, he said to Gladys. The buttercups nodded in the breeze and the petals of the daisies trembled. Yet farther off, across the field, they seemed stationary.

Gladys said, "Right now I could just about understand everything there is." Grainier knew how seriously she took her church and her Bible, and he thought she might be talking about something in that realm of things.

"Well, you see what I like," he said.

"Yes, I do," she said.

"And I see what I like very, very well," he said, and kissed her lips.

"Ow," she said. "You got my mouth flat against my teeth."

"Are you sorry?"

"No. Do it again. But easy does it."

The first kiss plummeted him down a hole and popped him out into a world he thought he could get along in—as if he'd been pulling hard the wrong way and was now turned around headed downstream. They spent the whole afternoon among the daisies kissing. He felt glorious and full of more blood than he was supposed to have in him.

When the sun got too hot, they moved under a lone jack pine in the pasture of jeremy grass, he with his back against the bark and she with her cheek on his shoulder. The white daisies dabbed the field so profusely that it seemed to foam. He wanted to ask for her hand now. He was afraid to ask. She must want him to ask, or surely she wouldn't lie here with him, breathing against his arm, his face against her hair—her hair faintly fragrant of sweat and soap . . . "Would you care to be my wife, Gladys?" he astonished himself by saying.

"Yes, Bob, I believe I would like it," she said, and she seemed to hold her breath a minute; then he sighed, and both laughed.

•

When, in the summer of 1920, he came back from the Robinson Gorge job with four hundred dollars in his pocket, riding in a passenger car as far as Coeur d'Alene, Idaho, and then in a wagon up the Panhandle, a fire was consuming the Moyea Valley. He rode through a steadily thickening haze of wood smoke into Bonners Ferry and found the little town crowded with residents from along the Moyea River who no longer had any homes.

Grainier searched for his wife and daughter among the folks sheltering in town. Many had nothing to do now but move on, destitute. Nobody had word of his family.

He searched among the crowd of some one hundred or so people camping at the fairgrounds among tiny collections of the remnants of their worldly possessions, random things, dolls and mirrors and bridles, all waterlogged. These had managed to wade down the river and through the conflagration and out the southern side of it. Others, who'd headed north and tried to outrun the flames, had not been heard of since. Grainier questioned everyone, but got no news of his wife and daughter, and he grew increasingly frantic as he witnessed the refugees' strange happiness at having got out alive and their apparent disinterest in the fate of anyone who might have failed to.

The northbound Spokane International was stopped in Bonners and wouldn't move on until the fire was down and a good rain had soaked the Panhandle. Grainier walked the twenty miles out along the Moyea River Road toward his home with a handkerchief tied over his nose and mouth to strain the smoke, stopping to wet it often in the river, passing through a silvery snow of ash. Nothing here was burning. The fire had started on the river's east side not far above the village of Meadow Creek and worked north, crossed the river at a narrow gorge bridged by flaming mammoth spruce trees as they fell, and devoured the valley. Meadow Creek was deserted. He stopped at the railroad platform and drank water from the barrel there and went quickly on without resting. Soon he was passing through a forest of charred, gigantic spears that only a few days past had been evergreens. The world was gray, white, black, and acrid, without a single live animal or plant, no longer burning and yet still full of the warmth and life of the fire. So much ash, so much choking smoke— it was clear to him miles before he reached his home that nothing could be left of it, but he went on anyway, weeping for his wife and daughter, calling, "Kate! Gladys!" over and over. He turned off the road to look in on the homesite of the Andersens, the first one past Meadow Creek. At first he couldn't tell even where the cabin had stood. Their acreage looked like the rest of the valley, burned and silent except for the collective hiss of the very last remnants of combustion. He found their cookstove mounding out of a tall drift of ashes where its iron legs had buckled in the heat. A few of the biggest stones from the chimney lay strewn nearby. Ash had buried the rest.

The farther north he hiked, the louder came the reports of cracking logs and the hiss of burning, until every charred tree around him still gave off smoke. He rounded a bend to hear the roar of the conflagration and see the fire a half mile ahead like a black-and-red curtain dropped from a night sky. Even from this distance the heat of it stopped him. He collapsed to his knees, sat in the warm ashes through which he'd been wading, and wept.

Ten days later, when the Spokane International was running again, Grainier rode it up into Creston, B.C., and back south again the evening of the same day through the valley that had been his home. The blaze had climbed to the ridges either side of the valley and stalled halfway down the other side of the mountains, according to the reports Grainier had listened to intently. It had gutted the valley along its entire length like a campfire in a ditch. All his life Robert Grainier would remember vividly the burned valley at sundown, the most dream-like business he'd ever witnessed waking—the brilliant pastels of the last light overhead, some clouds high and white, catching daylight from beyond the valley, others ribbed and gray and pink, the lowest of them rubbing the peaks of Bussard and Queen mountains; and beneath this wondrous sky the black valley, utterly still, the train moving through it making a great noise but unable to wake this dead world.

The news in Creston was terrible. No escapees from the Moyea Valley fire had appeared there.

Grainier stayed at his cousin's home for several weeks, not good for much, sickened by his natural grief and confused by the situation. He understood that he'd lost his wife and little girl, but sometimes the idea stormed over him, positively stormed into his thoughts like an irresistible army, that Gladys and Kate had escaped the fire and that he should look for them everywhere in the world until he found them. Nightmares woke him every night: Gladys came out of the black landscape onto their homesite, dressed in smoking rags and carrying their daughter, and found nothing there, and stood crying in the waste.

In September, thirty days after the fire, Grainier rented a pair of horses and a wagon and set out up the river road carting a heap of supplies, intending to put up shelter on his acre and wait all winter for his family to return. Some might have called it an ill-considered plan, but the experiment had the effect of bringing him to his senses. As soon as he entered the remains he felt his heart's sorrow blackened and purified, as if it were an actual lump of matter from which all the hopeful, crazy thinking was burning away. He drove through a layer of ash deep enough, in some places, that he couldn't make out the roadbed any better than if he'd driven through winter snows. Only the fastest animals and those with wings could have escaped this feasting fire.

After traveling through the waste for several miles, scarcely able to breathe for the reek of it, he quit and turned around and went back to live in town.

Not long after the start of autumn, businessmen from Spokane raised a hotel at the little railroad camp of Meadow Creek. By spring a few dispossessed families had returned to start again in the Moyea Valley. Grainier hadn't thought he'd try it himself, but in May he camped alongside the river, fishing for speckled trout and hunting for a rare and very flavorful mushroom the Canadians called morel, which sprang up on ground disturbed by fire. Progressing north for several days, Grainier found himself within a shout of his old home and climbed the draw by which he and Gladys had habitually found their way to and from the water.

He marveled at how many shoots and flowers had sprouted already from the general death.

He climbed to their cabin site and saw no hint, no sign at all of his former life, only a patch of dark ground surrounded by the black spikes of spruce. The cabin was cinders, burned so completely that its ashes had mixed in with a common layer all about and then been tamped down by the snows and washed and dissolved by the thaw.

He found the woodstove lying on its side with its legs curled up under it like a beetle's. He righted it and pried at the handle. The hinges broke away and the door came off. Inside sat a chunk of birch, barely charred. "Gladys!" he said out loud. Everything he'd loved lying ashes around him, but here this thing she'd touched and held.

He poked through the caked mud around the grounds and found almost nothing he could recognize. He scuffed along through the ashes and kicked up one of the spikes he'd used in building the cabin's walls, but couldn't find any others.

He saw no sign of their Bible, either. If the Lord had failed to protect even the book of his own Word, this proved to Grainier that here had come a fire stronger than God.

Come June or July this clearing would be grassy and green. Already foot-tall jack pine sprouted from the ashes, dozens of them. He thought of poor little Kate and talked to himself again out loud: "She never even growed up to a sprout."

Grainier thought he must be very nearly the only creature in this sterile region. But standing in his old homesite, talking out loud, he heard himself answered by wolves on the peaks in the distance, these answered in turn by others, until the whole valley was singing. There were birds about, too, not foraging, maybe, but lighting to rest briefly as they headed across the burn.

Gladys, or her spirit, was near. A feeling overcame him that something belonging to her and the baby, to both of them, lay around here to be claimed. What thing? He believed it might be the chocolates Gladys had bought in a red box, chocolates cupped in white paper. A crazy thought, but he didn't bother to argue with it. Once every week, she and the tyke had sucked one chocolate apiece. Suddenly he could see those white cups scattered all around him. When he looked directly at any one of them, it disappeared.

Toward dark, as Grainier lay by the river in a blanket, his eye caught on a quick thing up above, flying along the river. He looked and saw his wife Gladys's white bonnet sailing past overhead. Just sailing past.

He stayed on for weeks in this camp, waiting, wanting many more such visions as that of the bonnet, and the chocolates—as many as wanted to come to him; and he figured as long as he saw impossible things in this place, and liked them, he might as well be in the habit of talking to himself, too. Many times each day he found himself deflating on a gigantic sigh and saying, "A pretty mean circumstance!" He thought he'd better be up and doing things so as not to sigh quite as much.

Sometimes he thought about Kate, the pretty little tyke, but not frequently. Hers was not such a sad story. She'd hardly been awake, much less alive.

He lived through the summer off dried morel mushrooms and fresh trout cooked up together in butter he bought at the store in Meadow Creek. After a while a dog came along, a little red-haired female. The dog stayed with him, and he stopped talking to himself because he was ashamed to have the animal catch him at it. He bought a canvas tarp and some rope in Meadow Creek, and later he bought a nanny goat and walked her back to his camp, the dog wary and following this newcomer at a distance. He picketed the nanny near his lean-to.

He spent several days along the creek in gorges where the burn wasn't so bad, collecting willow whips from which he wove a crate about two yards square and half as tall. He and the dog walked to Meadow Creek and he bought four hens, also a rooster to keep them in line, and carted them home in a grain sack and cooped them up in the crate. He let them out for a day or two every now and then, penning them frequently so the hens wouldn't lay in secret places, not that there were many places in this destruction even to hide an egg.

The little red dog lived on goat's milk and fish heads and, Grainier supposed, whatever she could catch. She served as decent company when she cared to, but tended to wander for days at a time.

Because the ground was too bare for grazing, he raised his goat on the same laying mash he fed the chickens. This got to be expensive. Following the first frost in September he butchered the goat and jerked most of its meat.

After the second frost of the season, he started strangling and stewing the fowls one by one over the course of a couple of weeks, until he and the dog had eaten them all, the rooster, too. Then he left for Meadow

Creek. He had grown no garden and built no structure other than his lean-to.

As he got ready to depart, he discussed the future with his dog. "To keep a dog in town it ain't my nature," he told the animal. "But you seem to me elderly, and I don't think an elderly old dog can make the winter by your lonely up around these hills." He told her he would pay an extra nickel to bring her aboard the train a dozen miles into Bonners Ferry. But this must not have suited her. On the day he gathered his few things to hike down to the platform at Meadow Creek, the little red dog was nowhere to be found, and he left without her.

The abbreviated job a year earlier at Robinson Gorge had given him money enough to last through the winter in Bonners Ferry, but in order to stretch it Grainier worked for twenty cents an hour for a man named Williams who'd contracted with Great Northern to sell them one thousand cords of firewood for two dollars and seventy-five cents each. The steady daylong exertions kept him and seven other men warm through the days, even as the winter turned into the coldest seen in many years. The Kootenai River froze hard enough that one day they watched, from the lot where wagons brought them logs of birch and larch to be sawn and split, a herd of two hundred cattle being driven across the river on the ice. They moved onto the blank white surface and churned up a snowy fog that first lost them in itself, then took in all the world north of the riverbank, and finally rose high enough to hide the sun and sky.

Late that March Grainier returned to his homesite in the Moyea Valley, this time hauling a wagonload of supplies.

Animals had returned to what was left of the forest. As Grainier drove along in the wagon behind a wide, slow, sand-colored mare, clusters of orange butterflies exploded off the blackish purple piles of bear sign and winked and fluttered magically like leaves without trees. More bears than people traveled the muddy road, leaving tracks straight up and down the middle of it; later in the summer they would forage in the low patches of huckleberry he already saw coming back on the blackened hillsides.

At his old campsite by the river he raised his canvas lean-to and went about chopping down five dozen burned spruce, none of them bigger around than his own hat size, acting on the generally acknowledged theory that one man working alone could handle a house log about the circumference of his own head. With the rented horse he got the timber decked in his clearing, then had to return the outfit to the stables in Bonners Ferry and hop the train back to Meadow Creek.

It wasn't until a couple of days later, when he got back to his old home—now his new home—that he noticed what his labors had prevented his seeing: It was full-on spring, sunny and beautiful, and the Moyea Valley showed a lot of green against the dark of the burn. The ground about was healing. Fireweed and jack pine stood up about thigh high. A mustard-tinted fog of pine pollen drifted through the valley when the wind came up. If he didn't yank this crop of new ones, his clearing would return to forest.

He built his cabin about eighteen by eighteen, laying out lines, making a foundation of stones in a ditch knee-deep to get down below the frost line, scribing and hewing the logs to keep each one flush against the next, hacking notches, getting his back under the higher ones to lift them into place. In a month he'd raised four walls nearly eight feet in height. The windows and roof he left for later, when he could get some milled lumber. He tossed his canvas over the east end to keep the rain out. No peeling had been required, because the fire had managed that for him. He'd heard that fire-killed trees lasted best, but the cabin stank. He burned heaps of jack pine needles in the middle of the dirt floor, trying to change the odor's character, and he felt after a while that he'd succeeded.

In early June the red dog appeared, took up residence in a corner, and whelped a brood of four pups that appeared quite wolfish.

Down at the Meadow Creek store he spoke about this development with a Kootenai Indian named Bob. Kootenai Bob was a steady man who had always refused liquor and worked frequently at jobs in town, just as Grainier did, and they'd known each other for many years. Kootenai Bob said that if the dog's pups had come out wolfish, that would be quite strange. The Kootenais had it that only one pair in a wolf den ever made pups— that you couldn't get any of the he-wolves to mate except one, the chief of the wolf tribe. And the she-wolf he chose to bear his litters was the only bitch in the pack who ever came in heat. "And so I tell you," Bob said, "that therefore your wandering dog wouldn't drop a litter of wolves." But what if she'd encountered the wolf pack at just the moment she was coming into heat, Grainier wanted to know—might the king wolf have mounted her then, just for the newness of the experience? "Then perhaps, perhaps," Bob said. "Might be. Might be you've got yourself some dog-of-wolf. Might be you've started your own pack, Robert."

Three of the pups wandered off immediately as the little dog weaned them, but one, a dis-coordinated male, stayed around and was tolerated by its mother. Grainier felt sure this dog was got of a wolf, but it never even whimpered in reply when the packs in the distance, some as far away as the Selkirks on the British Columbia side, sang at dusk. The creature needed to be taught its nature, Grainier felt. One evening he got down beside it and howled. The little pup only sat on its rump with an inch of pink tongue jutting stupidly from its closed mouth. "You're not growing in the direction of your own nature, which is to howl when the others do," he told the mongrel. He stood up straight himself and howled long and sorrowfully over the gorge, and over the low quiet river he could hardly see across this close to nightfall . . . Nothing from the pup. But often, thereafter, when Grainier heard the wolves at dusk, he laid his head back and howled for all he was worth, because it did him good. It flushed out something heavy that tended to collect in his heart, and after an evening's program with his choir of British Columbian wolves he felt warm and buoyant.

He tried telling Kootenai Bob of this development. "Howling, are you?" the Indian said. "There it is for you, then. That's what happens, that's what they say: There's not a wolf alive that can't tame a man."

The pup disappeared before autumn, and Grainier hoped he'd made it across the line to his brothers in Canada, but he had to assume the worst: food for a hawk, or for the coyotes.

Many years later—in 1930—Grainier saw Kootenai Bob on the very day the Indian died. That day Kootenai Bob was drunk for the first time in his life. Some ranch hands visiting from across the line in British Columbia had managed to get him to take a drink by fixing up a jug of shandy, a mixture of lemonade and beer. They'd told him he could drink this with impunity, as the action of the lemon juice would nullify any effect of the beer, and Kootenai Bob had believed them, because the United States was by now more than a decade into Prohibition, and the folks from Canada, where liquor was still allowed, were considered experts when it came to alcohol. Grainier found old Bob sitting on a bench out front of the hotel in Meadow Creek toward evening with his legs wrapped around an eight-quart canning pan full of beer—no sign of lemonade by now—lapping at it like a thirsty mutt. The Indian had

been guzzling all afternoon, and he'd pissed himself re-
peatedly and no longer had the power of speech. Sometime after dark he wandered off and managed to get
himself a mile up the tracks, where he lay down uncon-
scious across the ties and was run over by a succession of
trains. Four or five came over him, until late next afternoon the gathering multitude of crows prompted someone to investigate. By then Kootenai Bob was strewn
for a quarter mile along the right-of-way. Over the next
few days his people were seen plying along the blank
patch of earth beside the rails, locating whatever little
tokens of flesh and bone and cloth the crows had missed
and collecting them in brightly, beautifully painted
leather pouches, which they must have taken off somewhere and buried with a fitting ceremony.

5

At just about the time Grainier discovered a rhythm to his seasons—summers in Washington, spring and fall at his cabin, winters boarding in Bonners Ferry—he began to see he couldn't make it last. This was some four years into his residence in the second cabin.

His summer wages gave him enough to live on all year, but he wasn't built for logging. First he became aware how much he needed the winter to rest and mend; then he suspected the winter wasn't long enough to mend him. Both his knees ached. His elbows cracked loudly when he straightened his arms, and something hitched and snapped in his right shoulder when he moved it the wrong way; a general stiffness of his frame worked itself out by halves through most mornings, and he labored like an engine through the afternoons, but he was well past thirty-five years, closer now to forty, and he really wasn't much good in the woods anymore.

When the month of April arrived in 1925, he didn't leave for Washington. These days there was plenty of work in town for anybody willing to get around after it. He felt like staying closer to home, and he'd come into possession of a pair of horses and a wagon—by a sad circumstance, however. The wagon had been owned by Mr. and Mrs. Pinkham, who ran a machine shop on Highway 2. He'd agreed to help their grandson Henry, known as Hank, an enormous youth in his late teens, certainly no older than his early twenties, to load sacks of cornmeal aboard the Pinkhams' wagon; this favor a result of Grainier's having stopped in briefly to get some screws for a saw handle. They'd only loaded the first two sacks when Hank sloughed the third one from his shoulder onto the dirt floor of the barn and said, "I am as dizzy as anything today," sat on the pile of sacks, removed his hat, flopped over sideways, and died.

His grandfather hastened from the house when Grainier called him and went to the boy right away, saying,

"Oh. Oh. Oh." He was open-mouthed with uncomprehension. "He's not gone, is he?"

"I don't know, sir. I just couldn't say. He sat down and fell over. I don't even think he said anything to complain," Grainier told him.

"We've got to send you for help," Mr. Pinkham said.

"Where should I go?"

"I've got to get Mother," Pinkham said, looking at Grainier with terror on his face. "She's inside the house."

Grainier remained with the dead boy but didn't look at him while they were alone.

Old Mrs. Pinkham came into the barn flapping her hands and said, "Hank? Hank?" and bent close, taking her grandson's face in her hands. "Are you gone?"

"He's gone, isn't he?" her husband said.

"He's gone! He's gone!"

"He's gone, Pearl."

"God has him now," Mrs. Pinkham said.

"Dear Lord, take this boy to your bosom . . ."

"You could seen this coming ever since!" the old woman cried.

"His heart wasn't strong," Mr. Pinkham explained.

"You could see that about him. We always knew that much."

"His heart was his fate," Mrs. Pinkham said. "You could looked right at him anytime you wanted and seen this."

"Yes," Mr. Pinkham agreed.

"He was that sweet and good," Mrs. Pinkham said. "Still in his youth. Still in his youth!" She stood up angrily and marched from the barn and over to the edge of the roadway—U.S. Highway 2—and stopped.

Grainier had seen people dead, but he'd never seen anybody die. He didn't know what to say or do. He felt he should leave, and he felt he shouldn't leave.

Mr. Pinkham asked Grainier a favor, standing in the shadow of the house while his wife waited in the yard under a wild mixture of clouds and sunshine, looking amazed and, from this distance, as young as a child, and also very beautiful, it seemed to Grainier. "Would you take him down to Helmer's?" Helmer was in charge of the cemetery and, with Smithson the barber's help, often prepared corpses for the ground. "We'll get poor young Hank in the wagon. We'll get him in the wagon, and you'll go ahead and take him for me, won't you? So I can tend to his grandmother. She's gone out of her mind."

Together they wrestled the heavy dead boy aboard the wagon, resorting after much struggle to the use of two long boards. They inclined them against the wagon's bed and flopped the corpse up and over, up and over, until it rested in the conveyance. "Oh—oh—oh—oh—" exclaimed the grandfather with each and every nudge. As for Grainier, he hadn't touched another person in several years, and even apart from the strangeness of this situation, the experience was something to remark on and remember. He giddyapped Pinkham's pair of old mares, and they pulled young dead Hank Pinkham to Helmer's cemetery.

Helmer, too, had a favor to ask of Grainier, once he'd taken the body off his hands. "If you'll deliver a coffin over to the jail in Troy and pick up a load of lumber for me at the yard on Main, then take the lumber to Leona for me, I'll pay you rates for both jobs separate. Two for the price of one. Or come to think of it," he said, "one job for the price of two, that's what it would be, ain't it, sir?"

"I don't mind," Grainier told him.

"I'll give you a nickel for every mile of it."

"I'd have to stop at Pinkham's and bargain a rate from them. I'd need twenty cents a mile before I saw a profit."

"All right then. Ten cents and it's done."

"I'd need a bit more."

"Six dollars entire."

"I'll need a pencil and a paper. I don't know my numbers without a pencil and a paper."

The little undertaker brought him what he needed, and together they decided that six and a half dollars was fair.

For the rest of the fall and even a ways into winter, Grainier leased the pair and wagon from the Pinkhams, boarding the mares with their owners, and kept himself busy as a freighter of sorts. Most of his jobs took him east and west along Highway 2, among the small communities there that had no close access to the railways.

Some of these errands took him down along the Kootenai River, and traveling beside it always brought into his mind the image of William Coswell Haley, the dying boomer. Rather than wearing away, Grainier's regret at not having helped the man had grown much keener as the years had passed. Sometimes he thought also of the Chinese railroad hand he'd almost helped to kill. The thought paralyzed his heart. He was certain the man had taken his revenge by calling down a curse that had incinerated Kate and Gladys. He believed the punishment was too great.

But the hauling itself was better work than any he'd undertaken, a ticket to a kind of show, to an entertainment composed of the follies and endeavors of his neighbors. Grainier was having the time of his life. He contracted with the Pinkhams to buy the horses and wagon in installments for three hundred dollars.

By the time he'd made this decision, the region had seen more than a foot of snow, but he continued a couple more weeks in the freight business. It didn't seem a particularly bad winter down below, but the higher country had frozen through, and one of Grainier's last jobs was to get up the Yaak River Road to the saloon at the logging village of Sylvanite, in the hills above which a lone prospector had blown himself up in his shack while trying to thaw out frozen dynamite on his stove. The man lay out on the bartop, alive and talking, sipping free whiskey and praising his dog. His dog's going for help had saved him. For half a day the animal had made such a nuisance of himself around the saloon that one of the patrons had finally noosed him and dragged him home and found his master extensively lacerated and raving from exposure in what remained of his shack.

Much that was astonishing was told of the dogs in the Panhandle and along the Kootenai River, tales of

rescues, tricks, feats of supercanine intelligence and hu-
manlike understanding. As his last job for that year,
Grainier agreed to transport a man from Meadow Creek
to Bonners who'd actually been shot by his own dog.

The dog-shot man was a bare acquaintance of Grainier's, a surveyor for Spokane International who came
and went in the area, name of Peterson, originally from
Virginia. Peterson's boss and comrades might have put
him on the train into town the next morning if they'd
waited, but they thought he might perish before then,
so Grainier hauled him down the Moyea River Road
wrapped in a blanket and half sitting up on a load of
half a dozen sacks of wood chips bagged up just to
make him comfortable.

"Are you feeling like you need anything?" Grainier
said at the start.

Grainier thought Peterson had gone to sleep. Or
worse. But in a minute the victim answered: "Nope.
I'm perfect."

A long thaw had come earlier in the month. The
snow was melted out of the ruts. Bare earth showed off
in the woods. But now, again, the weather was freezing,
and Grainier hoped he wouldn't end up bringing in a
corpse dead of the cold.

For the first few miles he didn't talk much to his

passenger, because Peterson had a dented head and crazy eye, the result of some mishap in his youth, and he was hard to look at.

Grainier steeled himself to glance once in a while in the man's direction, just to be sure he was alive. As the sun left the valley, Peterson's crazy eye and then his entire face became invisible. If he died now, Grainier probably wouldn't know it until they came into the light of the gas lamps either side of the doctor's house. After they'd moved along for nearly an hour without conversation, listening only to the creaking of the wagon and the sound of the nearby river and the clop of the mares, it grew dark.

Grainier disliked the shadows, the spindly silhouettes of birch trees, and the clouds strung around the yellow half-moon. It all seemed designed to frighten the child in him. "Sir, are you dead?" he asked Peterson.

"Who? Me? Nope. Alive," said Peterson.

"Well, I was wondering—do you feel as if you might go on?"

"You mean as if I might die?"

"Yessir," Grainier said.

"Nope. Ain't going to die tonight."

"That's good."

"Even better for *me*, I'd say."

Grainier now felt they'd chatted sufficiently that he might raise a matter of some curiosity to him. "Mrs. Stout, your boss's wife, there. She said your dog shot you."

"Well, she's a very upright lady—to my way of knowing, anyways."

"Yes, I have the same impression of her right around," Grainier said, "and she said your dog shot you."

Peterson was silent a minute. In a bit, he coughed and said, "Do you feel a little warm patch in the air? As if maybe last week's warm weather turned around and might be coming back on us?"

"Not as such to me," Grainier said. "Just holding the warm of the day the way it does before you get around this ridge."

They continued along under the rising moon.

"Anyway," Grainier said.

Peterson didn't respond. Might not have heard.

"Did your dog really shoot you?"

"Yes, he did. My own dog shot me with my own gun. Ouch!" Peterson said, shifting himself gently. "Can you take your team a little more gradual over these ruts, mister?"

"I don't mind," Grainier said. "But you've got to

get your medical attention, or anything could happen to you."

"All right. Go at it like the Pony Express, then, if you want."

"I don't see how a dog shoots a gun."

"Well, he did."

"Did he use a rifle?"

"It weren't a cannon. It weren't a pistol. It were a rifle."

"Well, that's pretty mysterious, Mr. Peterson. How did that happen?"

"It was self-defense."

Grainier waited. A full minute passed, but Peterson stayed silent.

"That just tears it then," Grainier said, quite agitated. "I'm pulling this team up, and you can walk from here, if you want to beat around and around the bush. I'm taking you to town with a hole in you, and I ask a simple question about how your dog shot you, and you have to play like a bunkhouse lout who don't know the answer."

"All right!" Peterson laughed, then groaned with the pain it caused him. "My dog shot me in self-defense. I went to shoot *him*, at first, because of what Kootenai

Bob the Indian said about him, and he slipped the rope. I had him tied for the business we were about to do." Peterson coughed and went quiet a few seconds. "I ain't stalling you now! I just got to get over the hurt a little bit."

"All right. But why did you have Kootenai Bob tied up, and what has Kootenai Bob got to do with this, anyways?"

"Not Kootenai Bob! I had the *dog* tied up. Kootenai Bob weren't nowhere near this scene I'm relating. He was before."

"But the *dog*, I say."

"And say I also, the *dog*. He's the one I ties. He's the one slips the rope, and I couldn't get near him—he'd just back off a step for every step I took in his direction. He knew I had his end in mind, which I decided to do on account of what Kootenai Bob said about him. That dog *knew* things—because of what happened to him, which is what Kootenai Bob the Indian told me about him—that animal all of a sudden *knew* things. So I swung the rifle by the barrel and butt-ended that old pup to stop his sass, and wham! I'm sitting on my very own butt end pretty quick. Then I'm laying back, and the sky is traveling away from me in the wrong direction. Mr. Grainier, I'd been shot! Right here!" Peterson pointed to the bandages around his left shoulder and chest. "By my own dog!"

Peterson continued: "I believe he did it because he'd been confabulating with that wolf-girl person. If she is a person. Or I don't know. A creature is what you can call her, if ever she was created. But there are some creatures on this earth that God didn't create."

"Confabulating?"

"Yes. I let that dog in the house one night last summer because he got so yappy and wouldn't quit. I wanted him right by me where I could beat him with a kindling should he irritate me one more time. Well, next morning he got up the wall and out through the window like a bear clawing up a tree, and he started working that porch, back and forth. Then he started working that yard, back and forth, back and forth, and off he goes, and down to the woods, and I didn't see him for thirteen days. All right. All right—Kootenai Bob stopped by the place one day a while after that. Do you know him? His name is Bobcat such and such, Bobcat Ate a Mountain or one of those rooty-toot Indian names. He wants to beg you for a little money, wants a pinch of snuff, little drink of water, stops around twice in every season or so. Tells me—you can guess what: Tells me the wolf-girl has been spotted around.

69

I showed him my dog and says this animal was gone thirteen days and come back just about wild and hardly knew me. Bob looks him in the face, getting down very close, you see, and says, 'I am goddamned if you hadn't better shoot this dog. I can see that girl's picture on the black of this dog's eyes. This dog has been with the wolves, Mr. Peterson. Yes, you better shoot this dog before you get a full moon again, or he'll call that wolf-girl person right into your home, and you'll be meat for wolves, and your blood will be her drink like whiskey.' Do you think I was scared? Well, I was. 'She'll be blood-drunk and running along the roads talking in your own voice, Mr. Peterson,' is what he says to me. 'In your own voice she'll go to the window of every person you did a dirty to, and tell them what you did.' Well, I know about the girl. That wolf-girl was first seen many years back, leading a pack. Stout's cousin visiting from Seattle last Christmas saw her, and he said she had a bloody mess hanging down between her legs."

"A bloody mess?" Grainier asked, terrified in his soul.

"Don't ask me what it was. A bloody mess is all. But Bob the Kootenai feller said some of them want to believe it was the afterbirth or some part of a wolf-child torn out of her womb. You know they believe in Christ."

"What? Who?"

"The Kootenais—in Christ, and angels, devils, and creatures God didn't create, like half-wolves. They believe just about anything funny or witchy or religious they hear about. The Kootenais call animals to be people. 'Coyote-person,' 'Bear-person,' and such a way of talking."

Grainier watched the darkness on the road ahead, afraid of seeing the wolf-girl. "Dear God," he said. "I don't know where I'll get the strength to take this road at night anymore."

"And what do you think?—I can't sleep through the night, myself," Peterson said.

"God'll give me the strength, I guess."

Peterson snorted. "This wolf-girl is a creature God didn't create. She was made out of wolves and a man of unnatural desires. Did you ever get with some boys and jigger yourselves a cow?"

"What!"

"When you was a boy, did you ever get on a stump and love a cow? They all did it over where I'm from. It's not unnatural down around that way."

"Are you saying you could make a baby with a cow, or make a baby with a wolf? You? Me? A person?"

Peterson's voice sounded wet from fear and passion. "I'm saying it gets dark, and the moon gets full, and there's creatures God did not create." He made a strangling sound. "God!—this hole in me hurts when I cough. But I'm glad I don't have to try and sleep through the night, waiting on that wolf-girl and her pack to come after me."

"But did you do like the Indian told you to? Did you shoot your dog?"

"No! *He* shot *me*."

"Oh," Grainier said. Mixed up and afraid, he'd entirely forgotten that part of it. He continued to watch the woods on either side, but that night no spawn of unnatural unions showed herself.

For a while the rumors circulated. The sheriff had examined the few witnesses claiming to have seen the creature and had determined them to be frank and sober men. By their accounts, the sheriff judged her to be a female. People feared she'd whelp more hybrid pups, more wolf-people, more monsters who eventually, logically, would attract the lust of the Devil himself and bring down over the region all manner of evil influence. The Kootenais, wedded as they were known to be to pagan and superstitious practice, would fall prey completely to Satan. Before the matter ended, only fire and blood would purge the valley . . .

But these were the malicious speculations of idle minds, and, when the election season came, the demons of the silver standard and the railroad land snatch took their attention, and the mysteries in the hills around the Moyea Valley were forgotten for a while.

6

Not four years after his wedding and already a widower, Grainier lived in his lean-to by the river below the site where his home had been. He kept a campfire going as far as he could into the night and often didn't sleep until dawn. He feared his dreams. At first he dreamed of Gladys and Kate. Then only of Gladys. And finally, by the time he'd passed a couple of months in solitary silence, Grainier dreamed only of his campfire, of tending it just as he had before he slept—the silhouette of his hand and the charred length of lodgepole he used as a poker—and was surprised to find it gray ash and butt ends in the morning, because he'd watched it burn all night in his dreams.

And three years later still, he lived in his second cabin, precisely where the old one had stood. Now he slept soundly through the nights, and often he dreamed of trains, and often of one particular train: He was on it; he could smell the coal smoke; a world went by. And then he was standing in that world as the sound of the train died away. A frail familiarity in these scenes hinted to him that they came from his childhood. Sometimes he woke to hear the sound of the Spokane International fading up the valley and realized he'd been hearing the locomotive as he dreamed.

Just such a dream woke him in December his second winter at the new cabin. The train passed northward until he couldn't hear it anymore. To be a child again in that other world had terrified him, and he couldn't get back to sleep. He stared around the cabin in the dark. By now he'd roofed his home properly, put in windows, equipped it with two benches, a table, a barrel stove. He and the red dog still bedded on a pallet on the floor, but for the most part he'd made as much a home here as he and Gladys and little Kate had ever enjoyed. Maybe it was his understanding of this fact, right now, in the dark, after his nightmare, that called

Gladys back to visit him in spirit form. For many minutes before she showed herself, he felt her moving around the place. He detected her presence as unmistakably as he would have sensed the shape of someone blocking the light through a window, even with his eyes closed.

He put his right hand on the little dog stretched beside him. The dog didn't bark or growl, but he felt the hair on her back rise and stiffen as the visitation began to manifest itself visibly in the room, at first only as a quavering illumination, like that from a guttering candle, and then as the shape of a woman. She shimmered, and her light shook. Around her the shadows trembled. And then it was Gladys—nobody else—flickering and false, like a figure in a motion picture.

Gladys didn't speak, but she broadcast what she was feeling: She mourned for her daughter, whom she couldn't find. Without her baby she couldn't go to sleep in Jesus or rest in Abraham's bosom. Her daughter hadn't come across among the spirits, but lingered here in the world of life, a child alone in the burning forest. But the forest isn't burning, he told her. But Gladys couldn't hear. Before his sight she was living again her last moments: The forest burned, and she had only a minute to gather a few things and her baby and run from the cabin as the fire smoked down the hill. Of what she'd snatched up, less and less seemed worthy, and she tossed away clothes and valuables as the heat drove her toward the river. At the lip of the bluff she held only her Bible and her red box of chocolates, each pinned against her with an elbow, and the baby clutched against her chest with both her hands. She stooped and dropped the candy and the heavy book at her feet while she tied the child inside her apron, and then she was able to pick them up again. Needing a hand to steady her along the rocky bluff as they descended, she tossed away the Bible rather than the chocolates. This uncovering of her indifference to God, the Father of All—this was her undoing. Twenty feet above the water she kicked loose a stone, and not a heartbeat later she'd broken her back on the rocks below. Her legs lost all feeling and wouldn't move. She was only able to pluck at the knot across her bodice until the child was free to crawl away and fend for itself, however briefly, along the shore. The water stroked at Gladys until by the very power of its gentleness, it seemed, it lifted her down and claimed her, and she drowned. One by one from eddy pools and from among the rocks, the baby plucked the scattered chocolates. Eighty-foot-long spruce jutting out over the water burned through and fell into the gorge, their clumps of green needles afire and trailing smoke like pyrotechnical snakes, their flaming tops hissing as they hit the river. Gladys floated past it all, no longer in the water but now overhead, seeing everything in the world. The moss on the shingled roof of her home curled and began to smoke faintly. The logs in the walls stressed and popped like large-bore cartridges going off. On the table by the stove a magazine curled, darkened, flamed, spiraled upward, and flew away page by page, burning and circling. The cabin's one glass window shattered, the curtains began to blacken at the hems, the wax melted off the jars of tomatoes, beans, and Canada cherries on a shelf above the steaming kitchen tub. Suddenly all the lamps in the cabin were lit. On the table a metal-lidded jar of salt exploded, and then the whole structure ignited like a match head.

Gladys had seen all of this, and she made it his to know. She'd lost her future to death, and lost her child to life. Kate had escaped the fire.

Escaped? Grainier didn't understand this news. Had some family downriver rescued his baby daughter? "But I don't see how they could have done, not unbeknownst to anybody. Such a strange and lucky turn would have made a big story for the newspapers—like it made for the Bible, when it happened to Moses."

He was talking out loud. But where was Gladys to hear him? He sensed her presence no more. The cabin was dark. The dog no longer trembled.

7

Thereafter, Grainier lived in the cabin, even through the winters. By most Januaries, when the snow had deepened, the valley seemed stopped with a perpetual silence, but as a matter of fact it was often filled with the rumble of trains and the choirs of distant wolves and the nearer mad jibbering of coyotes. Also his own howling, as he'd taken it up as a kind of sport.

The spirit form of his departed wife never reappeared to him. At times he dreamed of her, and dreamed also of the loud flames that had taken her. Usually he woke in the middle of this roaring dream to find himself surrounded by the thunder of the Spokane International going up the valley in the night.

But he wasn't just a lone eccentric bachelor who lived in the woods and howled with the wolves. By his own lights, Grainier had amounted to something. He had a business in the hauling.

He was glad he hadn't married another wife, not that one would have been easy to find, but a Kootenai widow might have been willing. That he'd taken on an acre and a home in the first place he owed to Gladys. He'd felt able to tackle the responsibilities that came with a team and wagon because Gladys had stayed in his heart and in his thoughts.

He boarded the mares in town during winters—two elderly logging horses in about the same shape and situation as himself, but smart with the wagon, and more than strong enough. To pay for the outfit he worked in the Washington woods one last summer, very glad to call it his last. Early that season a wild limb knocked his jaw crooked, and he never quite got the left side hooked back properly on its hinge again. It pained him to chew his food, and that accounted more than anything else for his lifelong skinniness. His joints went to pieces. If he reached the wrong way behind him, his right shoulder locked up as dead as a vault door until somebody freed it by putting a foot against his ribs and pulling on his arm. "It takes a great much of pulling," he'd explain to anyone helping him, closing his eyes and entering a darkness of bone torment, "more than that—pull harder—a great deal of pulling now, greater, greater, you just have to *pull* . . ." until the big joint unlocked with a sound between a pop and a gulp. His right knee began to wobble sideways out from under him more and more often; it grew dangerous to trust him with the other end of a load. "I'm got so I'm joined up too tricky to pay me," he told his boss one day. He stayed out the job, his only duty tearing down old coolie shacks and salvaging the better lumber, and when that chore was done he went back to Bonners Ferry. He was finished as a woodsman.

He rode the Great Northern to Spokane. With nearly five hundred dollars in his pocket, more than plenty to pay off his team and wagon, he stayed in a room at the Riverside Hotel and visited the county fair, a diversion that lasted only half an hour, because his first decision at the fairgrounds was a wrong one.

In the middle of a field, two men from Alberta had parked an airplane and were offering rides in the sky for four dollars a passenger—quite a hefty asking price, and not many took them up on it. But Grainier had to try. The young pilot—just a kid, twenty or so at the most, a blond boy in a brown oversuit with metal buttons up the front—gave him a pair of goggles to wear and boosted him aboard. "Climb on over. Get something under your butt," the boy said.

Grainier seated himself on a bench behind the pilot's. He was now about six feet off the ground, and already that seemed high enough. The two wings on either side of this device seemed constructed of the frailest stuff. How did it fly when its wings stayed still?—by making its own gale, evidently, driving the air with its propeller, which the other Albertan, the boy's grim father, turned with his hands to get it spinning.

Grainier was aware only of a great amazement, and then he was high in the sky, while his stomach was somewhere else. It never did catch up with him. He looked down at the fairgrounds as if from a cloud. The earth's surface turned sideways, and he misplaced all sense of up and down. The craft righted itself and began a slow, rackety ascent, winding its way upward like a wagon around a mountain. Except for the churning in his gut, Grainier felt he might be getting accustomed to it all. At this point the pilot looked backward at him, resembling a raccoon in his cap and goggles, shouting and baring his teeth, and then he faced forward. The plane began to plummet like a hawk, steeper and steeper, its engine almost silent, and Grainier's organs pushed back against his spine. He saw the moment with his wife and child as they drank Hood's Sarsaparilla in their little cabin on a summer's night, then another cabin he'd never remembered before, the places of his hidden childhood, a vast golden wheat field, heat shimmering above a road, arms encircling him, and a woman's voice crooning, and all the mysteries of this life were answered. The present world materialized before his eyes as the engine roared and the plane leveled off, circled the fairgrounds once, and returned to earth, landing so abruptly Grainier's throat nearly jumped out of his mouth.

The young pilot helped him overboard. Grainier rolled over the side and slid down the barrel of the fuselage. He tried to steady himself with a hand on a wing, but the wing itself was unsteady. He said, "What was all that durn hollering about?"

"I was telling you, 'This is a nosedive!'"

Grainier shook the fellow's hand, said, "Thank you very much," and left the field.

He sat on the large porch out front of the Riverside Hotel all afternoon until he found an excuse to make his way back up the Panhandle—an excuse in Eddie

Sauer, whom he'd known since they were boys in Bonners Ferry and who'd just lost all his summer wages in
bawdy environs and said he'd made up his mind to
walk home in shame.

Eddie said, "I was rolled by a whore."

"Rolled! I thought that meant they killed you!"

"No, it don't mean they killed you or anything. I
ain't dead. I only wish I was."

Grainier thought Eddie and he must be the same
age, but the loose life had put a number of extra years
on Eddie. His whiskers were white, and his lips puck-
ered around gums probably nearly toothless. Grainier
paid the freight for both of them, and they took the
train together to Meadow Creek, where Eddie might
get a job on a crew.

After a month on the Meadow Creek rail-and-ties
crew, Eddie offered to pay Grainier twenty-five dollars
to help him move Claire Thompson, whose husband
had passed away the previous summer, from Noxon,
Montana, over to Sandpoint, Idaho. Claire herself would
pay nothing. Eddie's motives in helping the widow were
easily deduced, and he didn't state them. "We'll go by
road number Two Hundred," he told Grainier, as if there
were any other road.

Grainier took his mares and his wagon. Eddie had his sister's husband's Model T Ford. The brother-in-law had cut away the rumble seat and built onto it a flat cargo bed that would have to be loaded judiciously so as not to upend the entire apparatus. Grainier rendez-voused with Eddie early in the morning in Troy, Mon-tana, and headed east to the Bull Lake road, which would take them south to Noxon, Grainier preceding by half a mile because his horses disliked the auto-mobile and also seemed to dislike Eddie.

A little German fellow named Heinz ran an auto-mobile filling station on the hill east of Troy, but he, too, had something against Eddie, and refused to sell him gas. Grainier wasn't aware of this problem until Eddie came roaring up behind with his horn squawking and nearly stampeded the horses. "You know, these gals have seen all kinds of commotion," he told Eddie when they'd pulled to the side of the dusty road and he'd walked back to the Ford. "They're used to anything, but they don't like a horn. Don't blast that thing around my mares."

"You'll have to take the wagon back and buy up two or three jugs of fuel," Eddie said. "That old schnitzel-kraut won't even talk to me."

"What'd you do to him?"

"I never did a thing! I swear! He just picks out a few to hate, and I'm on the list."

The old man had a Model T of his own out front of his place. He had its motor's cover hoisted and was half-lost down its throat, it seemed to Grainier, who'd never had much to do with these explosive machines. Grainier asked him, "Do you really know how that motor works inside of there?"

"I know everything." Heinz sputtered and fumed somewhat like an automobile himself, and said, "I'm God!"

Grainier thought about how to answer. Here seemed a conversation that could go no farther.

"Then you must know what I'm about to say."

"You want gas for your friend. He's the Devil. You think I sell gas to the Devil?"

"It's me buying it. I'll need fifteen gallons, and jugs for it, too."

"You better give me five dollars."

"I don't mind."

"You're a good fellow," the German said. He was quite a small man. He dragged over a low crate to stand on so he could look straight into Grainier's eyes. "All right. Four dollars."

"You're better off having that feller hate you," Grainier told Eddie when he pulled up next to the Ford with the gasoline in three olive military fuel cans.

"He hates me because his daughter used to whore out of the barbershop in Troy," Eddie said, "and I was one of her happiest customers. She's respectable over in Seattle now," he added, "so why does he hold a grudge?"

They camped overnight in the woods north of Noxon. Grainier slept late, stretched out comfortably in his empty wagon, until Eddie brought him to attention with his Model T's yodeling horn. Eddie had bathed in the creek. He was going hatless for the first time Grainier ever knew about. His hair was wild and mostly gray and a little of it blond. He'd shaved his face and fixed several nicks with plaster. He wore no collar, but he'd tied his neck with a red-and-white necktie that dangled clear down to his crotch. His shirt was the same old one from the Saturday Trade or Discard at the Lutheran church, but he'd scrubbed his ugly working boots, and his clean black pants were starched so stiffly his gait seemed to be affected. This sudden attention to terrain so long neglected constituted a disruption in the natural world, about as much as if the Almighty himself had been hit in the head, and Eddie well knew it. He behaved with a cool, contained hysteria.

"Terrence Naples has took a run at Mrs. Widow,"

he told Grainier, standing at attention in his starched pants and speaking strangely so as not to disturb the plaster dabs on his facial wounds, "but I told old Terrence it's going to be my chance now with the lady, or I'll knock him around the county on the twenty-four-hour plan. That's right, I had to threaten him. But it's no idle boast. I'll thrub him till his bags bust. I'm too horrible for the young ones, and she's the only go— unless I'd like a Kootenai gal, or I migrate down to Spokane, or go crawling over to Wallace." Wallace, Idaho, was famous for its brothels and for its whores, an occasional one of whom could be had for keeping house with on her retirement. "And I knew old Claire first, before Terrence ever did," he said. "Yes, in my teens I had a short, miserable spell of religion and taught the Sunday-school class for tots before services, and she was one of them tots. I think so, anyway. I seem to remember, anyway."

Grainier had known Claire Thompson when she'd been Claire Shook, some years behind him in classes in Bonners Ferry. She'd been a fine young lady whose looks hadn't suffered at all from a little extra weight and her hair's going gray. Claire had worked in Europe as a nurse during the Great War. She'd married quite late and been widowed within a few years. Now she'd sold her home and would rent a house in Sandpoint along the road running up and down the Idaho Panhandle.

The town of Noxon lay on the south side of the Clark Fork River and the widow's house lay on the north, so they didn't get a chance even to stop over at the store for a soda, but pulled up into Claire's front yard and emptied the house and loaded as many of her worldly possessions onto the wagon as the horses would pull, mostly heavy locked trunks, tools, and kitchen gear, heaping the rest aboard the Model T and creating a pile as high up as a man could reach with a hoe, and at the pinnacle two mattresses and two children, also a little dog. By the time Grainier noticed them, the children were too far above him to distinguish their age or sexual type. The work went fast. At noon Claire gave them iced tea and sandwiches of venison and cheese, and they were on the road by one o'clock. The widow herself sat up front next to Eddie with her arm hooked in his, wearing a white scarf over her head and a black dress she must have bought nearly a year ago for mourning; laughing and conversing while her escort tried to steer by one hand. Grainier gave them a good start, but he caught up with them frequently at the top of the long rises, when the auto labored hard and boiled over, Eddie giving it water from gallon jugs which the children—

boys, it seemed—filled from the river. The caravan moved slowly enough that the children's pup was able to jump down from its perch atop the cargo to chase gophers and nose at their burrows, then clamber up the road bank to a high spot and jump down again between the children, who sat stiff-armed with their feet jutting out in front, hanging on to the tie-downs on either side of them.

At a neighbor's a few hours along they stopped to take on one more item, a two-barreled shotgun Claire Thompson's husband had given as collateral on a loan. Apparently Thompson had failed to pay up, but in honor of his death the neighbor's wife had persuaded her husband to return the old .12 gauge. This Grainier learned after pulling the mares to the side of the road, where they could snatch at grass and guzzle from the neighbor's spring box.

Though Grainier stood very near them, Eddie chose this moment to speak sincerely with the widow. She sat beside him in the auto shaking the gray dust from her head kerchief and wiping her face. "I mean to say," Eddie said—but must have felt this wouldn't do. He opened his door quite suddenly and scrambled out, as flustered as if the auto were sinking in a swamp, and raced around to the passenger's side to stand by the widow.

"The late Mr. Thompson was a fine feller," he told

her. He spent a tense minute getting up steam, then went on: "The late Mr. Thompson was a fine feller. Yes."

Claire said, "Yes?"

"Yes. Everybody who knew him tells me he was an excellent feller and also a most . . . excellent feller, you might say. So they say. As far as them who knew him."

"Well, did you know him, Mr. Sauer?"

"Not to talk to. No. He did me a mean bit of business once . . . But he was a fine feller, I'm saying."

"A mean bit of business, Mr. Sauer?"

"He runned over my goat's picket and broke its neck with his wagon! He was a sonofabitch who'd sooner steal than work, wadn't he? But I mean to say! Will you marry a feller?"

"Which feller do you mean?"

Eddie had trouble getting a reply lined up. Meanwhile, Claire opened her door and pushed him aside, climbing out. She turned her back and stood looking studiously at Grainier's horses.

Eddie came over to Grainier and said to him, "Which feller does she *think* I mean? This feller! Me!"

Grainier could only shrug, laugh, shake his head.

Eddie stood three feet behind the widow and addressed the back of her: "The feller I mentioned! The one to marry! I'm the feller!"

She turned, took Eddie by the arm, and guided him back to the Ford. "I don't believe you are," she said. "Not the feller for me." She didn't seem upset anymore.

When they traveled on, she sat next to Grainier in his wagon. Grainier was made uncomfortable because he didn't want to get too near the nose of a sensitive woman like Claire Shook, now Claire Thompson—his clothes stank. He wanted to apologize for it, but couldn't quite. The widow was silent. He felt compelled to converse. "Well," he said.

"Well what?"

"Well," he said, "that's Eddie for you."

"That's not Eddie for *me*," she said.

"I suppose," he said.

"In a civilized place, the widows don't have much to say about who they marry. There's too many running around without husbands. But here on the frontier, we're at a premium. We can take who we want, though it's not such a bargain. The trouble is you men are all worn down pretty early in life. Are you going to marry again?"

"No," he said.

"No. You just don't want to work any harder than you do now. Do you?"

"No, I do not."

"Well then, you aren't going to marry again, not ever."

"I was married before," he said, feeling almost required to defend himself, "and I'm more than satisfied with all of everything's been left to me." He did feel as if he was defending himself. But why should he have to? Why did this woman come at him waving her topic of marriage like a big stick? "If you're prowling for a husband," he said, "I can't think of a bigger mistake to make than to get around me."

"I'm in agreement with you," she said. She didn't seem particularly happy or sad to agree. "I wanted to see if your own impression of you matched up with mine is all, Robert."

"Well, then."

"God needs the hermit in the woods as much as He needs the man in the pulpit. Did you ever think about that?"

"I don't believe I am a hermit," Grainier replied, but when the day was over, he went off asking himself, Am I a hermit? Is this what a hermit is?

Eddie became pals with a Kootenai woman who wore her hair in a mop like a cinema vamp and painted her lips sloppy red. When Grainier first saw them together, he couldn't guess how old she was, but she had brown, wrinkled skin. Somewhere she had come into possession of a pair of hexagonal eyeglasses tinted such a deep blue that behind them her eyes were invisible, and it was by no means certain she could see any objects except in the brightest glare. She must have been easy to get along with, because she never spoke. But whenever Eddie engaged in talk she muttered to herself continually, sighed and grunted, even whistled very softly and tunelessly. Grainier would have figured her for mad if she'd been white.

"She prob'ly don't even speak English," he said aloud, and realized that nobody else was present. He was all alone in his cabin in the woods, talking to himself, startled at his own voice. Even his dog was off wandering and hadn't come back for the night. He stared at the firelight flickering from the gaps in the stove and at the enclosing shifting curtain of utter dark.

8

Even into his last years, when his arthritis and rheumatism sometimes made simple daily chores nearly impossible and two weeks of winter in the cabin would have killed him, Grainier still spent every summer and fall in his remote home.

By now it no longer disturbed him to understand that the valley wouldn't slowly, eventually resume its condition from before the great fire. Though the signs of destruction were fading, it was a very different place now, with different plants and therefore with different animals. The gorgeous spruce had gone. Now came almost exclusively jack pine, which tended to grow up scraggly and mean. He'd been hearing the wolves less and less often, from farther and farther away. The coyotes grew numerous, the rabbits increasingly scarce. From long stretches of the Moyea River through the burn, the trout had gone.

Maybe one or two people wondered what drew him back to this hard-to-reach spot, but Grainier never cared to tell. The truth was he'd vowed to stay, and he'd been shocked into making this vow by something that happened about ten years after the region had burned.

This was in the two or three days after Kootenai Bob had been killed under a train, while his tribe still toured the tracks searching out the bits of him. On these three or four crisp autumn evenings, the Great Northern train blew a series of long ones, sounding off from the Meadow Creek crossing until it was well north, proceeding slowly through the area on orders from the management, who wanted to give the Kootenai tribe a chance to collect what they could of their brother without further disarrangement.

It was mid-November, but it hadn't yet snowed. The moon rose near midnight and hung above Queen Mountain as late as ten in the morning. The days were brief and bright, the nights clear and cold. And yet the nights were full of a raucous hysteria.

These nights, the whistle got the coyotes started, and then the wolves. His companion the red dog was out there, too—Grainier hadn't seen her for days. The chorus seemed the fullest the night the moon came full. Seemed the maddest. The most pitiable.

The wolves and coyotes howled without letup all night, sounding in the hundreds, more than Grainier had ever heard, and maybe other creatures too, owls, eagles—what, exactly, he couldn't guess—surely every single animal with a voice along the peaks and ridges looking down on the Moyea River, as if nothing could ease any of God's beasts. Grainier didn't dare to sleep, feeling it all to be some sort of vast pronouncement, maybe the alarms of the end of the world.

He fed the stove and stood in the cabin's doorway half-dressed and watched the sky. The night was cloudless and the moon was white and burning, erasing the stars and making gray silhouettes of the mountains. A pack of howlers seemed very near, and getting nearer, baying as they ran, perhaps. And suddenly they flooded into the clearing and around it, many forms and shadows, voices screaming, and several brushed past him, touching him where he stood in his doorway, and he could hear their pads thudding on the earth. Before his mind could say "these are wolves come into my yard," they were gone. All but one. And she was the wolf-girl.

Grainier believed he would faint. He gripped the doorjamb to stay on his feet. The creature didn't move, and seemed hurt. The general shape of her impressed him right away that this was a person—a female—a child. She lay on her side panting, a clearly human creature with the delicate structure of a little girl, but she was bent in the arms and legs, he believed, now that he was able to focus on this dim form in the moonlight. With the action of her lungs there came a whistling, a squeak, like a frightened pup's.

Grainier turned convulsively and went to the table looking for—he didn't know. He'd never kept a shotgun. Perhaps a piece of kindling to beat at the thing's head. He fumbled at the clutter on the table and located the matches and lit a hurricane lamp and found such a weapon, and then went out again in his long johns, barefoot, lifting the lantern high and holding his club before him, stalked and made nervous by his own monstrous shadow, so huge it filled the whole clearing behind him. Frost had built on the dead grass, and it skirled beneath his feet. If not for this sound he'd have thought himself struck deaf, owing to the magnitude of the surrounding silence. All the night's noises had stopped. The whole valley seemed to reflect his shock. He heard only his footsteps and the wolf-girl's panting complaint.

Her whimpering ceased as he got closer, approaching cautiously so as not to terrify either this creature or himself. The wolf-girl waited, shot full of animal dread and perfectly still, moving nothing but her eyes, following his every move but not meeting his gaze, the breath smoking before her nostrils.

The child's eyes sparked greenly in the lamplight like those of any wolf. Her face was that of a wolf, but hairless.

"Kate?" he said. "Is it you?" But it was.

Nothing about her told him that. He simply knew it. This was his daughter.

She stayed stock-still as he drew even closer. He hoped that some sign of recognition might show itself and prove her to be Kate. But her eyes only watched in flat terror, like a wolf's. Still. Still and all. Kate she was, but Kate no longer. Kate-no-longer lay on her side, her left leg akimbo, splintered and bloody bone jutting below the knee; just a child spent from crawling on threes and having dragged the shattered leg behind her. He'd wondered sometimes about little Kate's hair, how it might have looked if she'd lived; but she'd snatched herself nearly bald. It grew out in a few patches.

He came within arm's reach. Kate-no-longer growled, barked, snapped as her father bent down toward her, and then her eyes glassed and she so faded from herself he believed she'd expired at his approach. But she lived, and watched him.

"Kate. Kate. What's happened to you?"

He set down the lamp and club and got his arms beneath her and lifted. Her breathing came rapid, faint, and shallow. She whimpered once in his ear and snapped her jaws but didn't otherwise struggle. He turned with her in his embrace and made for the cabin, now walking away from the lamplight and thus toward his own monstrous shadow as it engulfed his home and shrank magically at his approach. Inside, he laid her on his pallet on the floor. "I'll get the lamp," he told her.

When he came back into the cabin, she was still there. He set the lamp on the table where he could see what he was doing, and prepared to splint the broken leg with kindling, cutting the top of his long johns off himself around the waist, dragging it over his head, tearing it into strips. As soon as he grasped the child's ankle with one hand and put his other on the thigh to pull, she gave a terrible sigh, and then her breathing slowed. She'd fainted. He straightened the leg as best he could and, feeling that he could take his time now, he whittled a stick of kindling so that it cupped the shin. He pulled a bench beside the pallet and sat himself, resting her foot across his knee while he applied the splint and bound it around. "I'm not a doctor," he told her. "I'm just the one that's here." He opened the window across the room to give her air.

She lay there asleep with the life driven half out of her. He watched her a long time. She was as leathery as an old man. Her hands were curled under, the back of her wrists calloused stumps, her feet misshapen, as hard and knotted as wooden burls. What was it about her face that seemed so wolflike, so animal, even as she slept? He couldn't say. The face just seemed to have no life behind it when the eyes were closed. As if the creature would have no thoughts other than what it saw.

He moved the bench against the wall, sat back, and dozed. A train going through the valley didn't wake him, but only entered his dream. Later, near daylight, a much smaller sound brought him around. The wolf-girl had stirred. She was leaving.

She leaped out the window.

He stood at the window and watched her in the

dawn effulgence, crawling and pausing to twist sideways on herself and snap at the windings on her leg as
would any wolf or dog. She was making no great speed
and keeping to the path that led to the river. He meant
to track her and bring her back, but he never did.

9

In the hot, rainless summer of 1935, Grainier came into a short season of sensual lust greater than any he'd experienced as a younger man.

In the middle of August it seemed as if a six-week drought would snap; great thunderheads massed over the entire Panhandle and trapped the heat beneath them while the atmosphere dampened and ripened; but it wouldn't rain. Grainier felt made of lead—thick and worthless. And lonely. His little red dog had been gone for years, had grown old and sick and disappeared into the woods to die by herself, and he'd never replaced her. On a Sunday he walked to Meadow Creek and hopped the train into Bonners Ferry. The passengers in the lurching car had propped open the windows, and any lucky enough to sit beside one kept his face to the sodden breeze. The several who got off in Bonners dispersed wordlessly, like beaten prisoners. Grainier made his way toward the county fairgrounds, where a few folks set up shop on Sunday, and where he might find a dog.

Over on Second Street, the Methodist congregation was singing. The town of Bonners made no other sound. Grainier still went to services some rare times, when a trip to town coincided. People spoke nicely to him there, people recognized him from the days when he'd attended almost regularly with Gladys, but he generally regretted going. He very often wept in church. Living up the Moyea with plenty of small chores to distract him, he forgot he was a sad man. When the hymns began, he remembered.

At the fairgrounds he talked to a couple of Kootenais—one a middle-aged squaw, and the other a girl nearly grown. They were dressed to impress somebody, two half-breed witch-women in fringed blue buckskin dresses with headbands dangling feathers of crow, hawk, and eagle. They had a pack of very wolfish pups in a feed sack, and also a bobcat in a willow cage. They took the pups out one at a time to display them. A man was just walking away and saying to them, "That dog-of-wolf will never be Christianized."

"Why is that thing all blue?" Grainier said.

"What thing?"

"That cage you've got that old cat trapped up in."

One of them, the girl, showed a lot of white in her, and had freckles and sand-colored hair. When he looked at these two women, his vitals felt heavy with yearning and fear.

"That's just old paint to keep him from gnawing out. It sickens this old bobcat," the girl said. The cat had big paws with feathery tufts, as if it wore the same kind of boots as its women captors. The older woman had her leg so Grainier could see her calf. She scratched at it, leaving long white rakes on the flesh.

The sight so clouded his mind that he found himself a quarter mile from the fairgrounds before he knew it, without a pup, and having seen before his face, for some long minutes, nothing but those white marks on her dark skin. He knew something bad had happened inside him.

As if his lecherous half-thoughts had blasted away the ground at his feet and thrown him down into a pit of universal sexual mania, he now found that the Rex

DENIS JOHNSON

Theater on Main Street was out of its mind, too. The display out front consisted of a large bill, printed by the local newspaper, screaming of lust:

One Day Only Thursday August 22
The Most Daring Picture of the Year
"Sins Of Love"
Nothing Like It Ever Before!

see Natural Birth
An Abortion
A Blood Transfusion
A Real Caesarian Operation
if you faint easily—don't come in!
trained nurses at each show

On the Stage—Living Models Featuring
Miss Galveston
Winner of the Famous Pageant of Pulchritude
In Galveston, Texas

No One Under 16 Admitted

Matinee
Ladies Only

Night
Men Only

In Person
Professor Howard Young
Dynamic Lecturer on Sex.
Daring Facts Revealed

The Truth About Love.
Plain Facts About Secret Sins
No Beating About the Bush!

Grainier read the advertisement several times. His throat tightened and his innards began to flutter and sent down his limbs a palsy which, though slight, he felt sure was rocking the entire avenue like a rowboat. He wondered if he'd gone mad and maybe should start visiting an alienist.

Pulchritude!

He felt his way to the nearby railroad platform through a disorienting fog of desire. *Sins of Love* would come August 22, Thursday. Beside the communicating doors of the passenger car he rode out of town, there hung a calendar that told him today was Sunday, August 11.

At home, in the woods, the filthiest demons of his nature beset him. In dreams Miss Galveston came to him. He woke up fondling himself. He kept no calendar, but in his very loins he marked the moments until Thursday, August 22. By day he soaked almost hourly in the frigid river, but the nights took him again and again to Galveston.

The dark cloud over the Northwest, boiling like an upside-down ocean, blocked out the sun and moon and stars. It was too hot and muggy to sleep in the cabin. He made a pallet in the yard and spent the nights lying on it naked in an unrelieved blackness.

After many such nights, the cloud broke without rain, the sky cleared, the sun rose on the morning of August 22. He woke up all dewy in the yard, his marrow thick with cold—but when he remembered what day had come, his marrow went up like kerosene jelly, and he blushed so hard his eyes teared and the snot ran from his nose. He began walking immediately in the direction of the road, but turned himself around to wander his patch of land frantically. He couldn't find the gumption to appear in town on this day—to appear even on the road to town for anyone to behold, thickly melting with lust for the Queen of Galveston and desiring to breathe her atmosphere, to inhale the fumes of sex, sin, and pulchritude. It would kill him! Kill him to see it, kill him to be seen! There in the dark theater full of disembodied voices discussing plain facts about secret sins he would die, he would be dragged down to Hell and tortured in his parts eternally before the foul and stinking President of all Pulchritude. Naked, he stood swaying in his yard.

His desires must be completely out of nature; he was the kind of man who might couple with a beast, or—as he'd long ago heard it phrased—jigger himself a cow.

Around behind his cabin he fell on his face, clutching at the brown grass. He lost touch with the world and didn't return to it until the sun came over the house and the heat itched in his hair. He thought a walk would calm his blood, and he dressed himself and headed for the road and over to Placer Creek, several miles, never stopping. He climbed up to Deer Ridge and down the other side and up again into Canuck Basin, hiked for hours without a break, thinking only: Pulchritude! Pulchritude!—Pulchritude will be the damning of me, I'll end up snarfing at it like a dog at a carcass, rolling in it like a dog will, I'll end up all grimed and awful with pulchritude. Oh, that Galveston would allow a parade of the stuff! That Galveston would take this harlot of pulchritude and make a queen of her!

At sunset, all progress stopped. He was standing on a cliff. He'd found a back way into a kind of arena enclosing a body of water called Spruce Lake, and now he looked down on it hundreds of feet below him, its flat surface as still and black as obsidian, engulfed in the shadow of surrounding cliffs, ringed with a double ring of evergreens and reflected evergreens. Beyond, he saw the Canadian Rockies still sunlit, snow-peaked, a hundred miles away, as if the earth were in the midst of its creation, the mountains taking their substance out of the clouds. He'd never seen so grand a prospect. The forests that filled his life were so thickly populous and so tall that generally they blocked him from seeing how far away the world was, but right now it seemed clear there were mountains enough for everybody to get his own. The curse had left him, and the contagion of his lust had drifted off and settled into one of those distant valleys.

He made his way carefully down among the boulders of the cliff, reaching the lakeside in darkness, and slept there curled up under a blanket he made out of spruce boughs, on a bed of spruce, exhausted and comfortable. He missed the display of pulchritude at the

Rex that night, and never knew whether he'd saved himself or deprived himself.

•

Grainier stayed at home for two weeks afterward and then went to town again, and did at last get himself a dog, a big male of the far-north sledding type, who was his friend for many years.

Grainier himself lived more than eighty years, well into the 1960s. In his time he'd traveled west to within a few dozen miles of the Pacific, though he'd never seen the ocean itself, and as far east as the town of Libby, forty miles inside Montana. He'd had one lover—his wife, Gladys—owned one acre of property, two horses, and a wagon. He'd never been drunk. He'd never purchased a firearm or spoken into a telephone. He'd ridden on trains regularly, many times in automobiles, and once on an aircraft. During the last decade of his life he watched television whenever he was in town. He had no idea who his parents might have been, and he left no heirs behind him.

Almost everyone in those parts knew Robert Grainier, but when he passed away in his sleep sometime in November of 1968, he lay dead in his cabin through the rest of the fall, and through the winter, and was never missed. A pair of hikers happened on his body in the spring. Next day the two returned with a doctor, who wrote out a certificate of death, and, taking turns with a shovel they found leaning against the cabin, the three of them dug a grave in the yard, and there lies Robert Grainier.

.

The day he bought the sled dog in Bonners Ferry, Grainier stayed overnight at the house of Dr. Sims, the veterinarian, whose wife took in lodgers. The doctor had come by some tickets to the Rex Theater's current show, a demonstration of the talents of Theodore the Wonder Horse, because he'd examined the star of it— that is, the horse, Theodore—in a professional capacity. Theodore's droppings were bloody, his cowboy master said. This was a bad sign. "Better take this ticket and go wonder at his wonders," the doctor told Grainier, pressing one of his complimentary passes on the lodger, "because in half a year I wouldn't wonder if he was fed to dogs and rendered down to mucilage."

Grainier sat that night in the darkened Rex Theater

amid a crowd of people pretty much like himself—his people, the hard people of the northwestern mountains, most of them quite a bit more impressed with Theodore's master's glittering getup and magical lariat than with Theodore, who showed he could add and subtract by knocking on the stage with his hooves and stood on his hind legs and twirled around and did other things that any of them could have trained a horse to do.

The wonder-horse show that evening in 1935 included a wolf-boy. He wore a mask of fur, and a suit that looked like fur but was really something else. Shining in the electric light, silver and blue, the wolf-boy frolicked and gamboled around the stage in such a way the watchers couldn't be sure if he meant to be laughed at.

They were ready to laugh in order to prove they hadn't been fooled. They had seen and laughed at such as the Magnet Boy and the Chicken Boy, at the Professor of Silly and at jugglers who beat themselves over the head with Indian pins that weren't really made of wood. They had given their money to preachers who had lifted their hearts and baptized scores of them and who had later rolled around drunk in the Kootenai village and fornicated with squaws. Tonight, faced with the spectacle of this counterfeit monster, they were silent at first. Then a couple made remarks that sounded like questions, and a man in the dark honked like a goose, and people let themselves laugh at the wolf-boy.

But they hushed, all at once and quite abruptly, when he stood still at center stage, his arms straight out from his shoulders, and went rigid, and began to tremble with a massive inner dynamism. Nobody present had ever seen anyone stand so still and yet so strangely mobile. He laid his head back until his scalp contacted his spine, that far back, and opened his throat, and a sound rose in the auditorium like a wind coming from all four directions, low and terrifying, rumbling up from the ground beneath the floor, and it gathered into a roar that sucked at the hearing itself, and coalesced into a voice that penetrated into the sinuses and finally into the very minds of those hearing it, taking itself higher and higher, more and more awful and beautiful, the originating ideal of all such sounds ever made, of the foghorn and the ship's horn, the locomotive's lonesome whistle, of opera singing and the music of flutes and the continuous moan-music of bagpipes. And suddenly it all went black. And that time was gone forever.

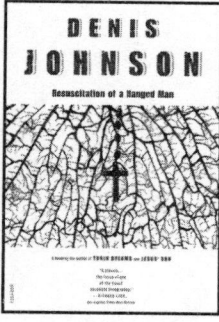